T0063992

The Last
Birdman

The Last Birdman

Mr. Mafia

authorHOUSE®

AuthorHouse™ LLC
1663 Liberty Drive
Bloomington, IN 47403
www.authorhouse.com
Phone: 1-800-839-8640

Published by AuthorHouse   02/10/2014

ISBN: 978-1-4918-4751-0 (sc)
ISBN: 978-1-4918-4755-8 (e)

Library of Congress Control Number: 2013923319

Any people depicted in stock imagery provided by Thinkstock are models, and such images are being used for illustrative purposes only. Certain stock imagery © Thinkstock.

This book is printed on acid-free paper.

Prelude

I was deep into a peaceful deep sleep when I heard the sound of my front door being kicked in. I jumped up from my sleep and quickly went for my Glock that was lying on the shelf in my closet. As I reached into the closet to grab my Glock, I heard footsteps running down the hallway towards the bedroom. My wife screamed and I quickly spun around in her direction and that's when I heard the shots going off. The bullet from the FNH 5.7 tore straight through my shoulder and it instantly spun me in a 360 degree turn. I dropped the Glock and fell over on to my side. A burning sensation rippled through my body and I nearly blacked out from the pain. As blood poured everywhere, I helplessly watched one guy smack my wife around like a ragdoll while another one tied her up to a chair. As I was going for my Glock, a third guy came through the door and shot me in the leg and I watched my leg get blown to the other side of the room. The third voice yelled out, for them to stop fucking around and help him with the big ass safe.

Chapter 1

GROWING UP IN NASHVILLE, Tennessee has its share of the good and its share of the bad, but mostly the good outweighs all the bad.

As a child all I ever wanted to do was become a police officer or lawyer when I grew up because the inner city, also known as the ghetto, was full of drug dealers, murderers, and prostitutes. In my little mind I thought I could be the one who could change my city or at least change my neighborhood.

My neighborhood is called Preston Taylor. It's a section of Cashville, Tennessee located on the west side of town. Every day I was forced to witness drug deals, shootings, gang activity, and sometimes murders. Mostly my mom would keep me inside the house. I wasn't allowed to play outside because she had to work and there was no one to supervise me while she was away. My oldest brother would watch me during the daytime when he wasn't running the streets; but mostly he would be on the corner, running to cars trying, to sell his dope. There were so many guys on each street corner of my neighborhood. I often wondered how everyone made money

My brother Je'Von was well known around the hood, all the people knew his M.O. He was a small time hustler with a hot trigger finger. He had been in numerous shoot-outs before he even turned seventeen. A few times the cops came to our house with warrants for shootings and sometimes it would be just to question him about a shooting. I always hated when the police would come to my house looking for my brother because I would be playing on the floor with my little Hot Wheel cars. The police would step on them and kick them over on purpose. There were never any nice policemen in my neighborhood. My mother would scream at the police to put the guns away because her eight year old (me) was in the house. They would quickly search the house and then leave. Sometimes the police would call my mother from work just to search her house for my brother because I would be there alone. They threatened to call Child Services on my mother.

Every other week or so, my mother would have to go to the rent office and explain to the project manager why the police kept coming to the house. Each and every time the police came to the house; my mother would have to listen to the project manager talk shit about evicting her from the projects. With the job my mother had, she couldn't afford to get evicted so finally she was forced to make the decision to remove Je'Von from her lease.

As the years went by I became older and wiser. I was fully determined not to be like my brother Je'Von. I was going to make something out of myself. If he wanted to be a thug and shoot people all of his life then that was his choice.

I had just finished high school in the year 2008 and I was planning to go to college at the University of Miami or a college in Atlanta, Georgia. My only problem was I didn't have enough money saved to complete the whole year, depending on which one I chose. I was already working at NTB (National Tire and Battery) as a tire technician so I just decided to take on a second job as a male stripper. I figured, how hard could it be to take my clothes off and shake my dick for some women that were willing to pay for some dick?

The night of my first try-out was a little bit different from what I expected but I made the cut. Right away the club owner explained that I should choose a stage name for myself and buy a couple of costumes. As I contemplated what I was going to call myself, a guy came up to me and started telling me where I could get my costumes tailored. He recommended that I go to Showtown, the Korean store on Murfreesboro Road. He gave me the card and the directions and then walked away. I packed my bags and headed to the store to see what kind of costumes they had to offer.

Once at the store, I noticed very quickly they had almost every kind of costume you could imagine. The Korean woman asked me what I was looking for. I told her I wasn't sure because I just started a new job that required me to dress up so I was checking out her selection. She asked if I was an exotic dancer. I told her yes and she escorted me to the selection that I would most likely be looking for. She informed me that they could make alterations to any of the costumes.

A couple of females walked into the store so she excused herself to help them. As I was looking through different racks of costumes, I picked up a bright red man's thong with glitter all along on the shaft. I instantly held it up to my crotch to see how it would look on me. As I was checking myself out, I was interrupted by a small giggle. I turned to see who it was and I saw a Korean girl that had to be around the age of eighteen. One look at her was enough for me to see that she was beautiful. I instantly put the thong down and ask her what was so funny. She replied, "You don't look like a stripper to me." I quickly told her that I didn't need to be cute to be a stripper because my dick was big enough to be a stripper. She started laughing and said, "Yeah right, I bet you have a teeny-weeny, tiny little dick."

I responded quickly that my teeny-weeny, tiny little dick was more than enough to bust her tight little pussy open. She tilted her head sideways and holla'd, "Yeah right, show me!" I said no because it would scare you and you will run to your little momma and tell her. She looked to the front of the store for her mother, then turned back to me and whispered, "Pull it out."

I said if I pulled my shit out it s going to cost you. She quickly told me that I was crazy and a Chicken Little boy. I told her I wasn't going to pull my shit out in the store but if she really wanted to know what I was working with then she could come over and grab it. At first she hesitated but then moved a little closer. I walked up to her and grabbed a handful of my dick so she could see it in my pants. She reached out to touch the bulge and I jumped back. She asked me if I was afraid. I told her I wanted fifty dollars if she wanted to touch it. She told me that she didn't have any money because her mother hadn't paid her yet. I quickly responded, "If you want to touch this big ole dick, then you better steal it out of the cash register or whatever it takes to get it." She told me she didn't steal so I told her, "Well that's too bad, you should start if you want to get this."

Before I walked away, I asked her for her name and her age. She told me her name was Cookie and she was eighteen about to turn nineteen. I told her when she turned nineteen to give me a call and just maybe I'd give her a big black birthday present with a bright red bow on it. I reached into my wallet and gave her one of my NTB business cards, "Call me sometimes, if you aren't scared." She smiled as she reached for the card with one hand and grabbed my dick with the other hand. I smiled and told her, "Yeah okay, now you owe me seventy-five dollars." She continued to hold my dick and said, "Hey, that's not fair, you said fifty dollars!" I smirked as I replied, "I want to purchase this thong and a black bow tie and when I see you again, I want my money or else." She pointed toward the front of the store and said, "My mother will ring it up at the front." Before I walked away, she asked, "Or else what?" I replied, "Or else I won't come back to this store." I laughed as I kept walking toward the counter where I paid for my items and walked out.

The very next day I had to work at NTB. I told my best friend Johnathon that I was going to be a stripper at Club Pussy Cat and a part-time stripper at Moon Glow. He started laughing, "Yeah right! I don't believe you!" I told him that I needed to make some money to pay for my fall college courses. He told me that I was crazy. I asked him how was I crazy and he said because you are trying to be a law student that strips on the side. I assured him that I only planned to strip for a few months or so.

After we finished talking and joking, we started working. All day he was messing with me when customers were not looking. After a long hard day of tire changing and shock removals, it was time to go home and get some rest.

Later that night I prepared for my first, official night at the club. When I got there I got very nervous so I decided to drink a few drinks to calm my nerves. I had never drunk alcohol before so I asked the bartender what drinks were popular. She told me, "Grey Goose vodka and orange juice, Ciroc vodka, and cranberry, Patron Shots, Hennessey and Coke." I didn't know the difference so told her to give me a Grey Goose and orange juice.

After my second cup, it was my time to hit the stage. I was waiting out back for the DJ to call me and one of the guys came up to me and asked me what I called myself. I hadn't thought about a name for myself so I quickly gave him the name Mandingo Red. The guy ran and told the DJ that my name was Mandingo Red and a few seconds later I heard the DJ screaming, "Ladies, please give it up for the amazing Mandingo Red!"

When I arrived on stage, I noticed the club was full of females and a few niggas were out in the audience. The Grey Goose had me right where I wanted to be so I easily tuned out the few faggot ass niggas that were there. The ladies loved my performance so much that I really got into it. Before I even thought about it, I pulled my dick out and shook it in a couple fat bitches' faces. They instantly went wild and started reaching for me and my dick. I backed up and the women started throwing and waving money. All of the ladies begged for me to come their way.

When my performance was over, I left the stage. I had money stuffed into my thong and in both of my boots. I headed to the bar to cop another Grey Goose and as I was waiting on my drink, a nigga walked up to the bar and tried to holla at me. I instantly kicked that nigga off of the stool and stomped his ass with my cowboy boots. The club owner ran out to see what was going on and a couple of bouncers had to pull me off of the dude. The bouncers picked the faggot up and escorted his ass out of the club and escorted me to the back of the club to a dressing room. The manager angrily told me that he wasn't going to tolerate fighting in his club because it was bad for business.

I didn't hesitate telling him I wasn't trying to fuck up his business, but I wasn't down with the gay ass shit. He told me to take it easy because being a stripper comes with some good and some bad. Just as I started to respond, I felt it coming. I started throwing up everywhere. I threw up all over him, the couch, and the floor. The boss man jumped up cursing and yelling, "You gonna pay for that couch to be cleaned and you gonna pay the cleaning bill for my clothes!" I apologized and I agreed that I indeed would cover the bill.

I sat down at the table hoping my head would stop spinning. As I got comfortable, I remembered that I hadn't counted my money. I pulled the money out of my thong and my boots and started counting. When I finished counting, I had made twelve hundred dollars. I searched for a pen to subtract my entry fee and other expenses like the dry cleaning for my boss and the upholstery cleaning for the couch. After I deducted one hundred and fifty dollars for the entry fee and an additional one hundred dollars for the cleaning, I thought to myself, not bad for one night's work.

The next morning, I was face down at the table with my money tightly balled up in my hand. I looked around my dressing room like, "Damn, what happened? Where am I?" I realized I was still at the club. I looked at my watch and I was twenty minutes late for work at NTB. I immediately called Johnathon and asked him to tell the boss that I would be an hour late. He said he would tell him and he would call me back to let me know what the boss said.

I rushed outside to the parking lot and jumped into my car and headed home to take a shower and change for work. I was speeding through the traffic on the highway as I was also searching for aspirin because my brain was throbbing with every heartbeat. I quickly discovered that I didn't have any so I decided to stop at the corner store once I got to my neighborhood. As I pulled into the parking lot I noticed some Crip niggas standing in the parking lot. I jumped out of the car and gave them the head signal for what's up. They looked at me and said, "What's up cuz?" while nodding back.

Before I could get to the door of the store, I heard bong, bong, bong. Gunshots rang out from a passing automobile. I laid down on the ground, trying not to get hit by the stray bullets. I crawled toward the door of the store. I looked back and saw two of the Crip niggas lying on the ground bleeding, and then all I heard was the other three Crip niggas returning gunfire back at the fleeing car. I crawled into the store, scared as hell and thanking the Lord for allowing me to live. By the time the gunshots stopped, I had forgotten what I even came to the store to get.

My head had stopped hurting and I felt a sharp pain and burning sensation in my arm. I reached to touch my arm and it was hurting worse when I moved it. There was blood on my shirt and I automatically began to panic. I shouted to the store man that I was shot and I needed an ambulance. He told me to have a seat and relax. I yelled out, "How the fuck am I supposed to relax when I'm bleeding to death?"

He approached me and gently raised my sleeve to get a better look at the wound. I asked him, "What in the fuck are you trying to do?" He responded, "Easy young buck, let me see the wound." He told me he would wrap it up to stop the bleeding until the ambulance arrived. As he was examining my arm, he started laughing at me. I asked him what was so fucking funny. He told me I had only been grazed by a bullet, not shot. I told him my arm was hurting like a bullet was in it, but he assured me that I wasn't hit. He walked up the aisle and brought me back some antibiotic ointment. He told me to let the paramedic check it out since they had to come get the two dead bodies lying in the parking lot. Around thirty-five minutes later, the paramedics showed up along with the coroner and several police cars. The paramedics looked at my arm and told me I had nothing to worry about but noted that I was lucky and I should be more careful in the future.

As I turned to let the homicide detective, Cliff Manning pass by, he stopped to question me about the shooting. I told him that it happened so fast, I didn't have a chance to even see what happened. He begged me to give him some details, but all I would say was I didn't know what happened. He made it clear that he could take me down to the station and hold me for questioning. I told him all I remember was getting out of my car and passing the two guys before they got killed. When I was passing them while heading to the door of the store, gunshots erupted from a passing car. He asked what kind of car, make, model, and color. I told him I wasn't sure because I was too busy crawling for the safety of the inside of the store.

He continued to press me for more details but I quickly told him that I didn't recall. He told me he knew I was lying and if I remembered anything else that could help, then give him a call. He handed me his business card and thanked me for my time. I apologized that I wasn't able to be more helpful then I jumped into my Regal and headed home to shower and change clothes.

Before I could get home, my boss from NTB called me throwing a fit because I was now almost two hours late for work. I explained to him the situation and he quickly lowered his voice and offered me the entire day off. I gladly accepted it because I knew I had to work at the club again later that night.

As usual when I got home, my mom wasn't there. She was at work trying to keep the bills paid. I walked into the house to loud ass music blaring. It was my brother playing the music and right away I recognized the tune. It was Young Buck's song Fuck Da World featuring Lyfe Jennings. I walked through the house singing the words of the song. My brother didn't hear me come in so I walked to his room to say what's up.

I stuck my head into the door and called his name but the music was too loud. I thought nothing of it so I continued into his room and grabbed him by the shoulder. As I grabbed his shoulder, he spun around, hit me in the nose with one fist, and held his Glock .45 in the other hand, aimed straight in my face. He blew weed smoke into my face and yelled over the music, "Damn nigga, you know betta than to sneak up on me like that. I coulda blown yo ass off the map!"

I went to get some toilet paper to stop the bleeding while he went to turn the music down. When I came back into the room I was expecting an apology but he never did give me one. His way of apologizing was asking me if I wanted to hit the blunt. I told him, "Hell no, I don't want to hit no damn blunt!" He replied by saying, "Nigga, this Dro!" I told him I didn't give a fuck about Dro, TIP, or nothing else then I turned and walked out.

I headed to my room to get my clothes and take a shower. As I gathered up all of my clothes, I rushed to the bathroom to get more tissue for my bleeding nose. I removed the tissue out of my nostril and re-stuffed it with a fresh piece. Before I decided to get into the bathtub, I decided to take a shit. As I sat there thinking just how quickly my day had already began to be fucked up, my brother knocked on the door and told me my cell phone was ringing. I told him to answer it and take a message. He answered it and holla'd through the door, "Man it's some girl name Cookie." I told him to slide the phone through the door and he did. I stopped the sliding phone with my foot, leaned over and picked it up. When I answered it I said, "What's up baby? Pimpjuice speaking." She didn't realize that it was me speaking so she said, "May I speak to Tre'Von?"

I said, "Yeah, this Pimpjuice, run yo mouth." She caught onto my voice and said, "Yeah right, you ain't no Pimpjuice!" I played it off and said, "Who this calling, Cookie Monster?"

"My name ain't no Cookie Monster, so stop playing," she responded

"Damn girl, you curse like a sailor, do you talk to your mother with dirty thang you call a mouth?" Before she could speak, I said, "Naw, I'm just playing. What's good Boo?"

"What are you doing besides talking out of the side of yo neck" Cookie asked?

"I'm in the bathtub playing with my dick cause yo sexy voice make my dick so so hard."

"Stop lying! You ain't playing with yo damn dick, so stop lying!"

"I'm serious girl; you got me rock hard with that sexy ass voice of yours. If you don't believe me, then let's Skype."

"I don't Skype, I have Tango. Do you get Tango on your phone," Cookie questioned?

"Naw bae, I ain't ever heard of that but I can check it out."

"Oooh, you such a lil freak, you lucky I like you though. Come over here, I have a present for you."

"I hope it's gonna be some of that Monica Lowenski!" I started laughing cause I knew she didn't understand that joke.

Cookie asked, "What is a Monica Lowenski and why you laughing? That shit wasn't funny!"

I responded, "Yeah that shit was funny. You ain't laughing cause you don't get it. Don't worry about it. I'll explain it later."

I asked her when and where she wanted to meet so she gave me the address and directions and told me to come over right away. She asked me if I knew where Thompson Lane was so I told her, of course. I told her that I would be there in thirty minutes so be expecting me. I started laughing when I heard her say, "You better show up or else." I quickly asked, "Or else what?"

"Or else I' ma track you down like a tiger and cut you up into tiny little pieces." We both laughed and said our good-byes to one another. I jumped into the bathtub and got so fresh and so clean. When I was done, I got dressed, stashed my gauop and bounced.

As I got close to Thompson Lane, I called and asked for the directions again. She quickly gave them to me and I said cool. As I pulled up to her house, I could see her standing in the screen door. I got out a car with a big smile. She opened the door and told me to come on in. Right away I noticed her little pink and white boy shorts and sleeveless tank top.

I told her she was looking good in her outfit. She thanked me and asked for a hug. I gave her one and made sure I checked out her ass. I was curious about how it felt so I squeezed it as I gave her a hug. Just as I thought, it wasn't big at all but it was firm with a little softness to it. I thought to myself, damn she got ass for a pretty little Korean girl, but I'ma have to help her fatten it up a lil mo.

As I was pulling away from her, she reached down and grabbed a hand full of my dick. I told her, "You now owe me a hundred and fifty dollars." Then I said, "All that grabbing is going to get you in trouble."

She laughed and Said, "I'm a big girl, I can handle whatever you can give."

I smiled and said, "Oh yeah, don't let your mouth overload yo ass and write a check that yo ass can't cash."

She was turning me on and she didn't even know it. I was ready to put my pound game on that pussy. I said to her, "You ain't ready to take a ride on this soul pole!"

She gave me a devilish grin and said, "Whatever, follow me. I got something special for you. Just as I was asking her what she had for me, she grabbed my hand and walked me to her bedroom. She told me to close my eyes and don't open them until she said so. I stood there with my eyes closed until she said it was okay to open them. As soon as I opened my eyes, she handed me three thongs and two G-strings like the ones male body builders wear. The thongs were different colors. The green one had rhinestones and buttons all over it, the blue one had some glow in the dark dollar signs on it, and the black one was all leather.

"This black one is hand stitched by me and the other three were done on the sewing machine. I also put the buttons and rhinestones on this one," Cookie explained. "It's a gift, from me to you but only on one condition."

"Oh yeah, what condition is that," I asked?

"I want to be the first one to get a lap dance. Go and put that black one on and let me see what the business is. I have never been to a strip club and I want to see you shake what yo momma gave ya!"

I laughed so hard my stomach was hurting and tears were coming out of my eye, but at the same time, I was becoming even more turned on and she didn't even know it.

I went to the bathroom and tried on the black leather thong. It was kind of small but I managed to get everything in it. I came out with the black thong on and her sexy slanted eyes lit up like a Christmas tree. I walked over to her and sat down in a chair and started teasing her with the dick. She got all excited and reached out for me but I quickly backed away from her. I started shaking my dick in front of her and she motioned with her index finger for me to come closer to her as she bit down on her bottom lip.

I could feel my dick starting to swell and I became more turned on. The harder I became, the tighter the thong began to get around my nuts. I was trying to pull it out a little to loosen it up, but when I pulled at it, the seam on the front busted open and the head of my dick fell out of the front of the thong.

Cookie instantly grabbed at it and begged to hold it. I stood closer to her with one leg up on the side of the chair and my other foot firmly planted on the floor. She had to use both hands to grab it. She lifted it up to get a better look at it. I just stood there and watched her act like a kid in a candy store. I wanted to see what she was going to do with it and in my mind I was screaming, "Do it! Do it! Gone and put it in yo mouth!"

Just the thought of what she might do with it made it get harder and harder. I got so hard that I could feel the pre cum working its way up the shaft. I tried to relax a little to hold it back. I started to ease away from her before things got sticky, but as I started pulling back; she tightened her grip and pulled me forward. Things were getting to the point of no return so I tried once again and she did the same thing. Before I could even say anything, my dick just started oozing pre cum right in her hands. Her face started to turn a bright pink color and her mouth gasped open. She squeezed the head of the dick and the sticky pre cum was everywhere.

She started caressing her titties with one hand and started stroking my dick with the other hand. I tilted my head back and let her work. As she stroked it a few more minutes, I could feel the mother load working itself up. I clenched my teeth and jaws together as I was very near a release. I took a deep breath and shot cum directly on her chin and watched as it dripped down onto her Juicy Couture tank top. As I shot my load, I couldn't take it any longer so I grabbed her and started pulling off her clothes. She whispered in my ear, "Come and get it."

She pulled off her cum drenched tank top and I started pulling down her boy shorts. Once she was out of her Hello Kitty thong, I became even more anxious. She had the prettiest shaved pussy that I had ever seen. I reached down to touch it to make sure it was real. Her hair was neatly trimmed into a landing strip. My dick began to get hard again as she dropped to her knees and put my swollen head straight into her mouth. I cocked my legs up on the bed so she could break me off. She licked the head a few times, and then she licked up and down the shaft. I wanted it in her mouth so I grabbed her hair and forced her head toward the dick. She licked it a couple of more times, then she started sucking it. I tilted my head back and closed my eyes as her tight little mouth clamped down around my swollen dick. I tried to force myself deeper within her throat but she started choking and gagging. Her mouth was so warm and tight that I just started fucking her mouth. She gagged and choked again but she didn't give up until I shot a second hot, sticky load deep down into her throat.

I stood her up and scooped her into my arms. She held onto my neck as I slid the dick in her dripping wet pussy and began to fuck her standing up. Her pussy was tighter than the O.J. Simpson glove and wetter than a swimming pool. Every time I stroked in and out of the pussy, it sounded like I was stirring macaroni and cheese. After twenty strokes or so, my knees started to get a little weak so I laid her down on the bed and told her to turn over on her hands and knees. Her pussy was so pink and pretty, I couldn't resist it so I started licking it from the back. She instantly started gripping the sheets and crawling away from me. As she crawled, I crawled with her, with my face deep into her pussy. It wasn't long before her pussy was dripping thick white fluid out of it. She reached down between her legs and stuck her fingers deep into her pussy. She looked me in the eyes, pulled her fingers out and started sucking and licking on her fingers. I was so hard that I motioned for her to come to me.

I laid back on the bed as she straddled me and attempted to ride me. I was able to glide my dick about half way into her and it wouldn't fit any further so I turned her over in the doggy-style position and tried to enter her that way. She was dripping wet, yet she was still so tight. I slowed down to take my time because I was becoming more and more anxious. I rubbed the head between her wet lips a few times then I slowly entered her. Once I was able to get the head in, I eased in and out until she loosened up. It took me about five minutes to get it halfway in then she started crawling away from me. I quickly grabbed her by the back of her neck and pushed her face down into the pillow. She was squirming and gripping the sheets as I fought to go deeper into her swollen wet pussy. I was about seventy-five percent deep into her when she collapsed on to her stomach. I asked her, "What's wrong baby girl?"

She rolled over and looked at me with her pretty slanted eyes and I could tell she had been crying. She said, "You're hurting me and I can't take it." I asked her if she wanted me to stop.

"She responded, "No, I'm a big girl, fuck my brains out!"

I asked, "Do you want to change position? This might be a little too much for you."

"Yes, let's change position cause you are much too rough," Cookie said.

Smiling at her, I said, "Okay baby, anything for you."

She wanted to get on top so she could control the depth and the speed of the sex. I happily laid back and let her climb on top.

She eased me back into her and slowly started rocking her hips as she rode me. I leaned into her body and started sucking her small but ample breast.

The more she gyrated and rocked the wetter she became and the more I eased deeper into her.

It felt so good to be inside her I could feel her pussy muscles contracting on my dick with every stoke.

Her rhythm sped up and so as her breathing. I knew she was preparing to come soon so I increased my speed to match hers. We rocked our hips in perfect harmony until she started climaxing. Once she started climaxing her speed started to decrease and I took over.

She laid her head on my chest so I wrapped my arms around her body and started jack hammering the pussy.

She went into a multiple organism as I continued to take her to the promise land.

After her third nut I came harder than a tidal wave and I was spent. We laid in one another arms cuddling and caressing each other.

Her body was smooth and soft; I laid there and admired every inch of its beauty. She was flawless in nature and pure in spirit.

I asked her to go and get me a hot wash towel so I could clean up with it. Once she returned she asked could she wash me up.

I explained to her that she had to be extra gentle with my balls because they are delicate and soft. She lathered up the wash cloth and started washing me so softly and gently. I could tell she was enjoying it because she took her time and washed me with great care. When she finished, she smiled and said okay I have one last gift for you. I asked her what it was and she handed me a hundred dollar bill.

I asked, "What is this for?"

"It's the fee you said I owed you for the grabbing it in the store."

I laughed then I said okay, now you owe me three hundred for everything we just did today. Before she could speak, I said and I want my money or else there will be problems. Cookie smiled and started laughing, asking, "Or else what? Don't make me whoop that ass!"

Her accent was so sexy and funny. I laughed and said, "Don't make me beat you with this billy club."

"What's a billy club, Cookie asked?

I grabbed a hand full of my dick then busted out laughing, "This big black billy stick!"

Chapter 2

LATER THAT NIGHT AROUND six thirty, I started rounding up all of the things that I wanted to take to the club then I left the house. I wasn't in a hurry because I knew I could get there within twenty minutes. Upon arrival, I stopped at the DJ booth to give him the CD's that I wanted him to play during my performance. I also stopped by the bar to say hello to Ms. Kitty's fine ass. My last stop was to let the owner know I would be stripping tonight. Of course he would want his dance fee up front, but that wasn't a problem because Cookie provided some of that earlier.

I went straight to my dressing room to try on my outfits. I was anxious to try on the new outfit that Cookie made for me. Trying the thong on made me think about Cookie's tight, wet pussy. My dick instantaneously became rock hard. I thought to myself, "Shit, she lucky that I'm trying to get my career off the ground because other than that, I would put a couple of babies up in her little slant-eyed ass." I was deep in thought to myself. Who would have known that Koreans got good ass pussy? I was really feeling good as I sat there with a dumb ass smile on my face.

My boss walked in and told me that I was up next to dance. I started singing in my head that 50 Cent song, *Magic Stick*. I decided that was going to be my motivation to hype me up before I went out on stage.

Once on stage, I danced to Young Buck's song, *Shawty Wanna Ride*. While the song was playing the hook and Buck was talking to Shawty, I did a slick little strip tease for the ladies. I removed my hat, my shirt, and my belt. Around the time the rapping started, I was in da chair stroking my dick for da ladies. I wanted to show them what Shawty wanted to ride!

The freaks in the audience started waving money and going crazy. A couple of fat bitches threw their panties on the stage. While shouting out, "Hell, I bet you won't let me ride that thang?" When the song got to the part where Buck tells Shawty don't be scared, show me what you got. I really acted a fool! I went to the edge of the stage so the ladies could see me good. I made sure my dick was rock hard. I dropped down and started doing push-ups. Every time I went down, my dick would touch the stage floor. The ladies went wild and started throwing dollars. I heard a couple of them shout out, "Work it honey, work it!" While a few shouted out, "Put that big ole thang on me!"

As soon as the song ended, I picked all of money up off of the stage and headed back to my dressing room. I was so amped up when I got back in the dressing room that I was talking to myself and smiling at the same time. I couldn't wait to go back on stage for my next song!

I decided to walk out to the bar and get a Ciroc and pineapple juice. Plus I wanted to see if April, the fine ass bartender, saw my performance. Once I got to the bar, I ordered my drink. Right away April prepared it and handed it to me. I didn't waste any time asking her if she saw my performance.

April responded, "Yeah, I caught a lil bit of it. Why you ask?"

I smiled and said, "So what did you think?"

She turned her nose up at me and dryly stated, "It was aight."

I played it cool and smiled, then I said, "Yeah, that's what's up, but don't be no hater."

April laughed, "Hater? You think so Boo Boo?"

I quickly said, "Yeah! Don't be fronting cause I can see in your eyes that you want me!"

She laughed even harder and simply said, "Yeah right nigga . . . in your wildest dreams!"

I said, "You couldn't handle me in my wildest dreams."

"Oh! Is that so lil boy? Well, let's just see what you got right here, right now, nigga!"

I told her to take a break and meet me in my dressing room, but she responded, "Naw nigga, fuck the dressing room! I want it right here, right now . . . on top of the bar!" We both started laughing at her comment. As I was about to say something back, two hood rat looking bitches walked up to the bar. One had blue hair and the other one had bright red hair, but she was thick as gumbo. Right away I peeped the fake Gucci purse and big ass Chanel earrings.

Off the top, the one with the blue hair spoke first. I tried to be nice and speak back but before I could get out a response, the one with the red hair said, "Aww nigga, you think you all that or something? You too good to speak to my girl?"

As I started to put her in check, April, the bartender, touched me on the shoulder and told me to be nice. I gave her a crazy look. She licked her tongue out at me and started laughing. Before I could react, April handed me a drink and told me the drink was on her. I started sipping my drink and I heard the thick red head say, "Damn nigga, you don't hear me talking to you? Don't act like you can't here cause I got enough money to buy yo stuck-up ass."

I turned around in my chair and looked her up and down, from head to toe and said, "Bitch, you don't have enough money to buy water so take that fake ass Gucci purse back up on Jefferson Street and tell Joe I said you need your ten dollars back!" Before she could speak, I said, "Take your ratchet looking ass on and play dead because you can't afford a high maintenance ass nigga like me!"

Her girl holla'd out, "Oh, no he didn't!" Before she could finish her sentence, Ms. Blue hair chimed right in with, "How much will it take to have yo sorry stuck-up ass?"

I turned in her direction and said, "Broke bitch! You need at least a band to even see me!

She rolled her eyes and jerked her neck in a half circle of a motion and said, "You out yo rabbit-ass mind if you think Im'a give you a band!"

I laughed at her and said, "Yeah, I know so take yo ghetto bird looking ass on and holla back after you boost a few more items and steal a few more checks! She got even madder and wanted to fight but I simply walked off and left them standing there talking shit. After all of the commotion, I realized it was almost time for me to go back on stage so I headed to my dressing room and changed outfits again.

Since it was getting close to my last performance, I wanted to go out with a bang. I decided to put on the leather G-string. I smiled as I checked myself out in the mirror. My nuts were hanging out and the tip of my dick was fully exposed. I could hear the sounds of Yo Gotti vibrate all thorough the club. My adrenaline started rushing and I started to become hyped. As soon as Yo Gotti went off, Lil Wayne and Future's song *Bitches Love Me* came on and I got even more hyper. As soon as I walked out on the stage, I noticed a lot of gay bitches hugged up with their bitches. Every time Lil Wayne said, "I could give a fuck about nothing as long as my bitches love me . . ." all the bitches started kissing.

The song, *Bands Will Make Her Dance*, came on the bitches went crazy. Money was flying everywhere and I started shaking that dick for the ladies. All of the women yelled out, "Bands will make him dance . . ." and I got super hyped as the money continued to fly!

When Miguel's song, *Adorn* started to come on, I started winding down my performance and went into my show stopper. I jumped off of the stage on to the platform with the ladies. I ripped my leather G-string off and walked through a small section of the crowd with my dick on showcase on top of a crisp white towel. The ladies went wild and everyone started waving their money and screaming, "Come here sexy!"

A thick redbone sista was waving her money while screaming, "Damn honey, bring that dick over to momma!" I stopped dead in front of her and looked directly into her pretty green eyes. I stroked my dick a few times while she watched. I gave her the "come here" signal with my finger. She rushed up to me with the quickness, but security stopped her before she got to me. I told security it was cool and to let her through. I told her that she was the lucky young lady to get on stage with me. I grabbed her hand and slowly walked her back to the stage.

I sat her down in a chair then gave her a lap dance. I put my dick directly up in her face, just inches away from her mouth and lips. I stroked it slowly while I gyrated my hips. She was in a trance as she watched my dick grow longer and fatter with each stroke. All she could do was follow my dick with her eyes with every move I made. I could see slob building up in the corners of her mouth. As I started backing up from her, she started reaching out. She waved a twenty dollar bill at me, so I walked back toward her. As I approached, she started throwing dollars. I stood directly over her and shook my dick at her. She reached out for the dick, but I grabbed her hands. I looked her in her eyes and helped her place her hands gently on my dick. I let her stroke it with me a few times, then I backed away from her.

As I turned toward the crowd, the rest of the women started throwing their money on stage while screaming, "Damn Daddy, pick me, I'm next!" One woman screamed out, "Damn, I love you!" While a few yelled out, "Bring that juicy dick over to me!"

The song ended and it was time for me to get off of the stage. I picked up my money and headed to the dressing room. I quickly changed clothes and counted my money because I was anxious to see how much I had made. As I finished counting, I said to myself, "Not bad for my second night of stripping."

I had made a grand and I was feeling real good. I went out to the bar to see if I could spot the redbone bitch. As I exited the dressing room, I thought to myself, "She would be just the person I would love to fuck tonight,". Bad as that bitch was, I would probably eat that pussy just to see how it taste. As I approached the bar, April was standing there smiling at me. I asked her what was so funny.

"You think you are God's gift to women, don't cha" April asked?

I laughed and said, "No, I don't, but you must."

Just as she started to speak, someone tapped me on my shoulder. I turned to see who it was and to my surprise, it was the green-eyed, redbone sista. I instantly smiled, but let out a cool, "What's up Red?"

As fast as the words came out of my mouth, she answered back, "You."

I said lets go some where and grab a bite to eat, She replied

"Naw nigga, fuck eating! Let's go back to my place."

I smiled and said, "Yeah, that's what I said . . . let me take you out to eat you."

She paid for my drink and we headed toward the door. Once we were standing in the parking lot, she asked me if I was riding with her or taking my car. I didn't want to take her car nor leave mine so I said ima follow you. At first we went back and forth, but then she finally agreed. We hopped into our cars and we were on our way. It only took fifteen minutes to reach her apartment complex. She lived off of Edmondson Pike in a gated community called Brentwood Downs. I pulled behind her car while she keyed her code to open the gate.

Once I was sitting comfortably on her leather sectional, I realized I didn't even know her name. I looked around the neatly, well furnished apartment, then quickly asked, "So what's yo name, Sexy Red?"

"My name is Diamond. What's yours?"

I smiled and said, "Tre'Von." I really didn't care, but I asked anyway, "Where yo man at?"

"I don't have a man. I'm as single as a dollar bill," she answered.

"Why is a sexy woman like you single," I asked?

"Has anyone ever told you that you talk too much? You are turning me off with the questions," she responded.

Before I could respond, she started taking off my clothes. I started helping her get my clothes off so she stepped back and started watching. After she finished admiring my body, she grabbed me by the hand and escorted me to her bedroom. When we reached the bed, she pushed me down on it and started undressing herself. I told her to turn the lights on so I could watch. She turned the bedside lamp on and went back to undressing. I was immediately turned on because she really knew how to give a good strip tease. Her body was so smooth and tight. She had thick thighs, a small waist, and a flat stomach that revealed her stomach muscles.

I wanted to ask her what she did for a living because her body was very well kept. I could tell she worked out at least twice a week, if not more. Just watching her strip out of her clothes made me want to beat that pussy all night. After she was totally undressed, she did a model pose, and then said so what do You think?

I quickly answered, "Damn baby, I'm impressed!"

Diamond told me to make myself comfortable while she freshened up. I couldn't control myself so I tried to play it cool. I watched her ass sway from side to side with every step she took toward the bathroom door. Before she could disappear through the door, I had pre cum leaking down my leg.

She yelled through the bathroom door, "Just make yourself comfortable. I got some juice, tea, water, and Kool-Aid in the refrigerator, if you want something to drink." Once I heard the shower running, I went to the kitchen and made me a cup of orange juice and came back to the bedroom.

As I was waiting, I started jacking off so I could get that first nut out of the way. I didn't want to be a one-minute man. I wanted to be fully ready to stand up in the pussy all night. After I came, I went to the bathroom and wiped off with tissue. Since she was still in the shower, I pulled the shower curtain back and asked if I could join her. She smiled and said yes, so I stepped on in.

"Would you like a wash cloth to wash with," Diamond asked?

I replied, "Naw sexy, I'm good. How about you wash me up the one you're using?" She washed me up and I washed her.

We got out of the shower and started drying off. As I walked out of the bathroom, she laid across the bed in the spread-eagle position. She motioned with her finger for me to come to her. I wasted no time diving in head first. I kissed her neck, breast, collarbone and nipples as she grabbed the remote control and hit a button. Just then, R Kelly's song, *Your Body's Calling*, came through the speakers nice and clear.

I smiled to myself but I kept on kissing and licking down her stomach. She laid back and enjoyed my work so I began to get cockier by the second. I licked and kissed down her thigh until I reached her feet. I started sucking on her pretty red toes, one at a time. Once I was done with all ten of them, I headed upwards between her inner thighs and slowly kissed until my lips met with her lips. Her pussy was wetter than Niagara Falls so I parted them open and started licking in an eight motion around her clit.

She moaned, "Oh yeah, that's the spot," while pulling my hair and shoving my face deeper in her pussy. I slid two fingers inside of her and fingered her while I started to suck her swollen clit. I rubbed the upper front wall of vagina, giving her the "come here" signal with my fingers. After many minutes of that, she couldn't take it any longer. Between deep breaths, she was telling me that she was cumming.

She tightened her legs around my neck and I applied more pressure to her clit and she went wild. She arched her back and her eyes rolled to the back of her head. I could feel her pussy starting to pulsate in my mouth as she grabbed a hand full of my braids and started pulling them. The more her pussy started pulsating, the more she started gyrating all over my face. She let out a loud moan, then fell flat to the bed. I looked up at her and her face was a bright red.

After she regained her breath, she turned me over on my back and started returning the favor. Since I had already gotten off, I knew that it was going to take a minute or so before I got off again. I laid back and watched her deep throat every inch of my dick, all the way down to the balls. After a few gags, she started sucking with no hands. I was surprised she could fit me all the way down her throat. She wrestled with it like it was an anaconda.

She sucked my dick like she was the one who invented the art of dick sucking. She started licking my balls and I started squirming. She licked up and down the side of my dick like it was an ice cream stick. I was all the way turned on so I told her to get on top of it and ride it like a cow girl. She deep throated me a few more times, hoping I would cum but I never did so she hopped on top of me. Her pussy was wet but so tight at the same time. I worked myself inside her and she instantly started gyrating her hips to a slow pace rhythm. She started doing tricks on the dick, I watched her turn around backwards with my dick still in her then ride it backwards.

I said, "Turn around and let me see those beautiful eyes."

She replied, "No you just want to see my sex faces." The more she worked, the wetter she became, and the harder I became. Her pussy got so wet that it started making that farting sound all I could do was hold on and enjoy the ride because she was riding the dick like a true horse rider. The pussy got so good I started throwing my dick to her with every stroke, finally we caught the same rhythm and we were in perfect balance. We both rocked our hips and bodies to our very own music and it was a wonderful game or give and take until I pulled back to far and slid out. Her pussy was so wet I had pussy juice all the way up on my stomach and down my legs. I was completely covered in her love juice and it felt good.

I flipped her off of me and instructed her to lay on her back. She happily laid back and spread her legs wide open. I lifted her legs up and placed them onto my shoulders as she stuffed me deep inside her I started long stroking at a nice pace until she started clawing the skin off of my back.

Soon as the sweat hit my tender back I instantly felt the burn and I couldn't take it any longer so I stopped stroking. She said "Baby why you stop?" I replied, "My back is on fire from all that scratching you were doing." She apologized and begged me not to stop.

I said, "Okay sexy, lets switch position to doggy style." I went deep back up in her and she cried that I was being too rough. I eased up just a bit and continued digging deep within her. After five minutes of non-stop beating I was just about to get my second nut when I felt a sharp blow to the back of my head and blood shot everywhere. I instantly fell to the floor and was out like a light.

I woke up to the sound and pain of my head being stomped into the floor. As soon as I came to my senses, I instantly grabbed my head and that's when I felt the blows shift to my ribs and side. My face was covered in blood and I couldn't see, but I knew that it had to be more than one person beating and assaulting me.

I heard Diamond screaming and crying. She asked them to stop, but I heard a voice ordering her to shut the fuck up before you get it to. Diamond begged for them to please don't, but then the guy said, "Bitch I should kill yo funky ass for even fucking with this nigga!"

By the time the kicking stopped, I was half unconscious and halfway out of it. I heard the clicking sound of what sounded like a gun but I was too helpless to move. A heard a voice say, "Drag his bitch ass out to the trunk of the car cause he is going for a ride."

As the guy started dragging me by my legs, I heard Diamond yell out, "Stop it Eric! I'm going to call the police on you and Shawn." I heard a loud slapping noise and then she fell to the floor next to me. They ran out of the apartment and she crawled over to me and attempted to help me to my feet. Right away I fell over onto the bed because I couldn't stand. She rushed to the bathroom and got a wet towel to wash away the blood. Just as she gently started wiping the blood off of my face, I heard a window break and my car alarm started to sound off. She ran to her bedroom window and said, "Oh shit! They just set your car on fire."

The next time I woke up again, I was in Vanderbilt Hospital in the ICU. At first, I didn't know where I was but as soon as I moved, the pain shot through my side like I had been hit with a Mack truck. I was looking for the nurse but I didn't know how to reach her, so I just pulled the I.V. out of my arm. A beeping bell went off on the monitor and a couple of nurses ran into the room to see what was going on.

One nurse came over and stuck the I.V. back into my arm and right away I grunted from the pain. She smiled and said, "Welcome back Mr. Lockridge, I see that you're finally awake." I said which hospital am I in and how long have I been here?" She said you are in Vanderbilt Hospital and you have been in a comma for two and a half days now.

I asked, "How did I get here and what day is it?" She responded a young woman brought You in and dropped you off so fast that no one was able to get her information or ask what had happened to You. The nurse turned and asked, "Are you hungry?" I told her I was starving and she told me she was sure I was hungry because I had been eating through a tube for the last two days.

She started towards the door then turned and said, "I'm about to notify your family to let them know that you are awake and we will get you something to eat up here." Twenty minutes later the nurse was bringing me some food I tried to sit up in my bed but my side was killing me. The nurse rushed over to show me how to raise the bed up, as she did so I started staring down her shirt. I had a big smile on my face as I stared at her pretty white Laced bra. My mind instantly wondered off to, 'damn I wonder if she has on matching panties?' She must have caught me staring cause she quickly closed her jacket and stood straight up.

I apologized to her and she smiled but quickly turned and walked out. I watched her ass sway from side to side as she was leaving and I thought to myself damn what a sexy walk she has. She looked back over her shoulder to see if I was looking then quickly walked out the door.

As she was going out I noticed my mother and brother coming in the same door. I instantly smiled and waved for them to come on in. My mother had tears in her eyes and my brother eyes was blood shot red so I knew what he had been doing. My mother cried, "Oh my baby" over and over and my brother was giving me the eye from behind my mother's back. I assumed that he had something to say that he didn't want her to hear so I frowned up with the expression of pain. She quickly ask me if I needed her to go and get the nurse and I told her it was okay, but I asked her if she could please go to the cafeteria and get me some hot wings. With no hesitation, she got right up and did so. My brother didn't waste any time in asking, "Who did this to you bro?"

I responded, "Damn bro I don't even know. All I remember is the name Eric."

"Eric who? What the nigga look like and do you know where he be at?"

"I don't know bruh, didn't get to see the nigga's face cause he busted me over the head from behind and I was dazed from the first blow. The bitch that I was with have to know that nigga cause she was screaming for the nigga to stop and she called him by his name."

"What bitch and what's her name lil' bruh?"

I said, "All I know is Diamond. I met her at the club and we went back to her house for a fuck fest. Shit was all good the first hour or so then that's when this fucked up shit happened."

The situation didn't look good because I was sitting in ICU with three broken ribs, a concussion, and thirty stitches in the back of my head and on top of that I didn't have a clue about who Eric was and what Diamond's last name was. Just as I started to tell Je'von to fuck it, it came to me. I smiled and said, "Yo bro, I don't have the answers that you are looking for but I do remember that bitch apartment and the apartment number."

He looked at me with a scandalous looking smile then said, "What is it bro?"

As I opened my mouth to speak, my mother was entered into the room, so Je'Von quickly shot me a don't-say-nothing-in-front-of-moms look. My mom looked at me and said, "Tre'Von who is Cookie?" I told her Cookie was a good friend of mine, I asked her why was she was asking.

"Oh I just asked baby cause she has been calling you nonstop for the last two days."

I asked, "Do you have my phone with you cause I don't have it?"

"Yes your phone is right here baby; the nurse gave me all your money and your phone."

She went into her purse and pulled out my cell phone and soon as she had it in her hand she said, "Now Tre, you know that you aren't supposed to be using this in here." I asked Ma to just give me the phone and chill out. Before she could speak, I said, "Oh yea, I'm good so don't be missing any more days from work on the account of me and I'ma be alright so please stop worrying." She looked at me and shook her head and then told me You just want to talk on that damn phone. She went on to say, "Don't tell me that you are alright, cause you need to put that damn phone down and get you some rest."

"I'm good Ma so stop worrying and go back to work. I have been in a comma for the last two days so I'm good on rest. She threw her hands up and walked out. I told Je'von that I would talk to him later and we would finish our conversation. He gave me some dap then headed for the door. I quickly called up Cookie to see what was going on with her. Cookie wanted to know what happened and asked if I was alright. I told her that it was long story and I didn't want her to worry about it all because I was fine. Just as I was about to get into a good conversation with her, two nurses walked in and told me that I was being moved to my own room. I told Cookie that I was about to be moved to my own room so I would call her back. The nurses wheeled me out and down the hall to the elevator.

We rode until we were on the eighth floor and then they took me to room eight twenty-five. I called Cookie back and we talked for an hour or so and then she finally asked if she could come up and see me. I told her yeah she could come, but only if she promised not to wear panties. She said I was crazy and she wasn't leaving the house without panties on. I told her to take them off in the car or in the bathroom. She laughed and said, "We'll see. I will be there in thirty minutes."

I fell asleep shortly after I hung up the phone with Cookie. I must have been dreaming about being in Diamond's house because my mind kept playing back to the night I was jumped on. I instantly woke up and looked around and that's when I noticed Cookie sitting beside my bed, holding my hand. I asked her how long she had been sitting there and she told me she hadn't been there very long but long enough to see that I was having a bad dream. She told me that I had nothing to fear because she'd be there for me. I asked her if she was going to protect me. And she looked me in my eyes and told me yes and then she gave me a kiss on the forehead.

I told her not to get anything started that she couldn't finish. She looked at me and laughed. I asked her what was so funny. She told me she had been worried sick about me but now that she was there with me, she knew I was alright. She said I was still the freak with the big mouth.

I said, "Oh yeah, is that how you feel?" She said she was just playing but she asked me how I really felt. I told her that I would be doing better if she would give me another kiss and she leaned in and gave me a kiss. As she kissed me, I slid my hand up her skirt. I said, "Damn, I thought I told you not to wear any panties." She gave me a devilish grin and said, "I couldn't leave out of the house without my panties on, but I still thought about you."

"How did you think about me if you got on panties?" I asked. She grabbed my hands, opened her legs, and pushed my hands up to her crotch. As my finger went deep inside her pussy, she told me she had on crotch-less panties just for me. I said, "Who you calling the freak? You the freaky one! You know I need to see it." She responded, "You know it's going to cost you fifty dollars just to see it."

I laughed, "Yeah, that's how you feel? Fifty huh? If I pay you fifty, I want to touch it, see it, and eat it." She smiled a big bright smile and I told her to get in the bed with me.

As she started to get in the bed with me, I tried to slide over and a sharp pain shot through my ribs and the rest of my body. She immediately grabbed my hand and asked if I was alright. I told her I was good but I didn't think it was a good idea for her to get in the bed with me. She looked kind of disappointed, but then she said she had a better idea. She stuck her hand down in my gown and started stroking my dick. Right away I got hard so I just laid back and closed my eyes and enjoyed the wonderful feeling. I whispered to her not to stop. Just as I said that, she stopped.

I asked, "Why you stop?" She responded, "I got a better idea baby." I asked, "What could be better than this?" She stood and started walking toward the door. I asked her where are you going? "That ain't no better idea!" I said. She looked over her shoulder and told me to relax for a moment and said I'll be right back, I watched her walk through the door and leave. I laid there with a hard dick, wondering where in the fuck she went, but no sooner than she left, she had returned with a cup in hand. I asked, "What's in the cup?"

She responded, "You ask too many questions, just lay back and close your eyes." I said, "Yeah okay, just hurry up and show me your great idea." She pulled the covers back and she whispered, "No peeping," and then I felt something cold touch my body. I instantly jerked and pain shot through my ribs. I let out a grunt of pain and she quickly apologized. I felt her rub the ice down my chest and to my stomach. She then pulled the covers down a bit further. I started peeping, but I acted like I wasn't. I watched her put an ice cube in her mouth with one hand and with the other hand she stroked on my dick.

Once I was all the way hard, she started giving me head with the ice in her mouth. The ice was cold, so I jumped when I first felt the ice on my dick. The pain shot through my ribs again, but this time it was well worth it. The head was so good that I told Cookie to turn her ass toward my face so I could play with her pussy. I stuck two fingers in her tight little pussy and started fucking her. She got wetter and wetter. As I fingered her deeper, she sucked faster and harder. I watched her pussy get so wet as my fingers went in and out of her pretty pussy.

I couldn't take it any longer, so I withdrew my fingers out of her and stuck them deep into my mouth. The pussy tasted so good, so I told her to slide back towards me a little bit. I wasted no time sticking my whole face deep into her creamy pussy. I started licking her and I could feel myself about ready to explode. I fought to hold back, but I just couldn't hold it. I licked her three more times and she went down two more times on me and I exploded and shot cum all in her mouth and throat. I moaned from the pressure that was being released and also from the pain in my ribs.

She looked back at me with cum dripping from the corner of her mouth. I watched her swallow all of my love juices and take her tongue to lick the remaining cum from the corner of her mouth. She then said in a sweet and sex tone, "Do you feel better now?" I struggled to regain my breath so I laid there and just shook my head in a yes, yes, yes motion. She smiled a big bright smile showing nothing but pretty white teeth. She wanted to play nurse and washed me up so I let her give me a sponge bath. When she finished, she asked me if I wanted to watch the Titans game. I said I don't really care much for the Titans but fuck it I'll watch anything with you after what you just did.

She turned the T.V on and the game but it was three minutes before halftime. Tennessee was winning, 28—21. Jack Locker had thrown the ball for three touchdowns and two hundred and seventy yards. Once halftime started, the cheerleaders ran out on the field. I started watching the cheerleaders do their thang and that's when I noticed her. It was Diamond or a woman that looked just like Diamond. I thought my eyes were playing tricks on me so I did a double take. All I could do was stare at the T.V and say un fucking believable!

I sat there with my eyes glued to the television until the halftime show was over. I quietly watched the game with Cookie, but my mind was deep in thought. I couldn't wait to tell Je'Von what I had just learned. After the game went off, I told Cookie I was getting tired. She said she understood. She gave me a kiss, said she would call me later and headed for the door. I watched her walk to the door, looking so good. She turned, waved good-bye, and then she was gone.

A few hours later the nurse came by to check on me and to also tell me that the doctor would be by to see me the next day. She informed me that if the doctor liked what he saw on the x-ray then he would sign me out to go home. Although my ribs were still hurting, that was good news for me to hear. I was anxious to go home, but most importantly I was anxious to go the next Tennessee Titans game . . . to pay someone a special visit.

The very next day, the doctor came to see how my head was. He sent me down the hall to get my head scanned. The scan showed that my brain was fine and the swelling had left completely. After viewing the x-ray for my head and my ribs, the doctor decided that I should remain in the hospital for at least another three days. I assured him that I felt fine but he didn't want to take any chances. Since the accident, I hadn't thought to call my boss to tell him why I hadn't been to work in the last three and a half days. As soon as the doctor left the room, I called over to my job to inform my boss of the news.

My boss's phone rang two times and his secretary answered. She quickly let me know that he wasn't in the office. I told her who I was and she said, "Oh yeah, I was wondering when you were going to call?" She then went on to say that I was fired and I could come pick up my last check. I explained the situation to her but she simply said she would relay the message but she couldn't guarantee anything, then she hung up the phone.

I laid there in the bed feeling so disgusted that all I could do was think about how in the hell had my life turned to shit in less than one week? I thought, "Damn, I nearly got shot in a drive by, my brother Je'Von busted my nose by accident, I met a beautiful redbone bitch that I fucked and got my ass beat for, my car got blown up, and now on top of it all, I just lost the only legal job that I had. I was scared to ask myself what else could possibly go wrong and that's when I looked up and noticed that she was standing directly in front of me. Right away I thought I was hallucinating so I just stared without saying a word.

Finally, she spoke, "How are you? Are you okay?"

I said I'm making it but I feel like shit and it was getting worst by the minute. She apologized for what happened, but I didn't want to hear no I'm-sorry-shit. "I thought you said that you didn't have a man," I questioned? Before I allowed her to respond, I lost my composure and I began to yell, "On top of that, this nigga has a fucking key to your apartment!"

She responded, "He must have made an extra key before he returned the original one."

"That's some bullshit! Who don't get their locks changed after a break-up?

She begged, "You have got to believe me. What I'm telling you is the truth. He's obsessed with me and he doesn't want to accept that it's over!"

I said, "Shit! Believe you? Believing you is what got my head cracked, ribs broken, and my car blown up!"

"I'm sorry and I'll do whatever I can to help you get another car," Diamond said.

I responded in a calmer tone, "Okay Diamond. By the way, what is your name, Diamond what?"

"Lewis, my name is Diamond Lewis."

"How can I believe you and I don't even know you, Diamond," I asked?

"But you do know my name and you know where I live. That's a start isn't it?"

"Yeah," I said, "but where do you work and how are you gonna help me to get to another car?"

She responded, "I work for Bellsouth and I have an office downtown Nashville."

"Bitch, quit lying! You are a cheerleader for the Titans and Lewis probably ain't your real last name neither!" She told me she had to go because she was now late for work. Then she said I' ma come back to see you later. Before I could speak, she rushed out of the room and vanished right before my eyes.

I really needed to find out more about her so called ex-boyfriend, Eric. I wish my brother Je'Von was up here so he could have put that bitch in the trunk and make her talk. I picked up the telephone and dialed 411 for Information. Once the operator came on the line, I asked for the Tennessee Titan football headquarters. The number was given to me so I hung up and dialed the number. An automated voice message came on and delivered a list of selections and options for each office extension. I carefully listened to all of the choices then I pressed star as I waited. The phone rang four times, and then a woman answered. I told the lady that I was Detective Mills calling to verify information on a cheerleader by the name of Diamond Lewis. The woman put me on hold. When she returned to the line, she informed me that there was a Diamond on the squad, but her last name was Jones. I asked if they had a headshot. She confirmed and then asked if I wanted to come over to view it, I asked her could she email it to me. She agreed to attach the photo to an email and send it to me. I thanked the lady for her help and gave her my email address.

Before she hung up, the lady asked me if Diamond was in any kind of trouble. I explained that I wasn't at liberty to discuss details and that I only wanted to speak with her. I informed the lady that she shouldn't disclose our conversation to anyone until a positive ID was made of the young lady in question.

Two days later, the doctor came in and told me that I could be discharged from the hospital. He prescribed some pain killers for my ribs after wrapping them with bandages.

I dialed my brother and told him to come get me. He said he'd be there in five minutes. I said cool and hung up. I gathered up all of my belongings and headed to the elevator. As I waited on the elevator to arrive, I saw a sexy nurse come through and I couldn't stop staring. The elevator finally came up and I hopped on and rode it down to a super crowded lobby. Everyone was watching T.V. while some kids were running all around, and some were crying. I thought to myself, "This is a madhouse!"

I decided to step outside to wait for Je'Von. It felt good to be out there. The weather was beautiful, the air smelled fresh, and the breeze felt good across my skin. Just as I thought about how wonderful it felt, I heard loud music coming up the block. I looked down the street but I saw nothing. Two seconds later, I saw my brother's box Chevy turn the corner. I was thinking, "Damn, why he got to have his music up so loud, knowing these crackers will call the police on him for that shit." He pulled up and I walked to the car and slowly began to get inside.

As I was getting into the car, I noticed he had a blunt in the ash tray and a pistol on the seat. As we pulled away from the hospital, I reached over and the turned the music down because I wasn't in no mood to hear no Lil Boosie Bad Azz. Je'Von looked at me crazy so I asked, "What?" He stared real hard for a minute and asked me what I remembered about that bitch and that nigga Eric. I immediately told him he was on some bullshit.

Je'Von responded, "Bullshit? Nigga what you mean? This 'bullshit' has to be handled, nigga! Retaliation is a must!"

I said, "Whatever!"

"Whatever my ass, Tre'Von! Listen man, you got to go hard out here in these streets cause they will eat you up and spit you out!"

I questioned, "What movie you get that from?"

"You think everything is a motherfucking game, Tre. It's real in the field. You let a nigga do that type of shit to you once, then he will do it again and before you know it, you dead and mamma crying. Then you'll look stupid!"

"If I'm dead, Jay, how I'm gone look stupid?"

Je'Von was beyond anger, "Man, what the fuck do you know about that nigga?"

I just exhaled, "Man, I'll tell you later after I check something out that may be helpful."

He looked at me like he wanted to fight, but he pulled his blunt from the ashtray, lit it up, and said, "Yo Tre, you want to hit this Sour Diesel?"

"Sour what?" Je'Von just shook his head and turned the radio back up to full crank and bobbed his head to the music of Webbie and Lil Boosie Bad Azz. I fanned the smoke away from my face, hoping like hell that we would get to the house as quick as possible.

He stopped at 400 Degrees Chicken and got us something to eat, and then we headed back out West to the projects in the neighborhood that we call home. All I wanted to do was relax and figure out what I was going to do about a car and a new job. I needed money for Law School and since I had three broken ribs, working at the strip club was out of the question for the time being.

Chapter 3

WE PULLED UP AT the crib so I got out of the car and walked into the house. I was starving and the chicken that I was holding smelled way too good. At the crib I kicked back with my feet on the table. I turned on the T.V., put my phone on the charger because I needed to check for that email, and I ate my chicken. One hour later, my cellphone started ringing. I answered and it was Johnathon. Thirty-five minutes into our conversation, the other line started beeping. I stared at the phone number, but I couldn't remember whose number it was. I told Johnathon that I would call him back and I clicked over and said hello.

A sexy, intriguing voice spoke over the phone and as quickly as I was interested, I instantly became disinterested when I realized the voice was Sasha's, my ex-girlfriend. I hadn't heard from her in four months so right away I wondered what she wanted. Before I could speak, she started telling me just how much she missed me, needed me, and loved me. I wasn't in the mood for her usual lies and games so I laughed and told her to cut the bullshit. I asked, "Sasha, what do you really want?"

She paused for a brief moment, and then she finally said, "I'm in some trouble and I need to borrow three hundred dollars."

I just shook my head to myself and asked, "Why don't you go suck some dope boy's dick? That's what you seem to like, right? Dope boys, right?"

She got mad and started raising her voice and started using vulgar words, but I wasn't in the mood for her stupid hostility so I pressed the end-call button right in her face. I started watching T.V. again but my ribs were starting to hurt so I popped the medication that the doctor prescribed for me. Forty-five minutes later, I was fast asleep on the couch in the living room.

I had awakened to a brand new day. I didn't have a job, I didn't have a car. I had nowhere to be and nowhere to go. I decided to call Cookie to see how she was doing. She was super surprised to hear my voice when she answered the phone. I said, "Hello Sexy. How are you? Guess who is out of the hospital?"

She was talking a mile a minute so I waited on her to slow down before I decided to ask her if she was coming by to see me. She said she had a surprise for me, but couldn't come by until she finished working. I was cool with that so I told her to hit me up when she was on her way over. She said she would call soon and then she said, "Tre, I love you." I got really quiet for a moment because that caught me off guard. Without really thinking, I responded, "I love you to Cookie." I hung up the phone and I was mad at myself for telling her that. I knew that I didn't really mean what I had just said, it just came out wrong. I decided that I would just tell her that I was on some really strong medication and I shouldn't be held responsible for my words and actions. How could she love me after only a few weeks? We had only fucked three times so I knew that it was impossible for her to love me this soon. I decided I was just going to overlook what she said.

As I was coming out of deep thought, my cousin Black was walking through the door. He sat down on the couch and asked me what was crackin? I told him not a damn thang, but no money and mo problems. He threw a box of Swishers at me and said roll up nigga. He said two or three blunts of this will solve all of yo problems. I wished I could believe that, but I just looked at him like he was crazy because I knew it wasn't true. I tossed the cigars back to him and I told him that I would pass. He happily smiled and said, "Shit! That's just more for me. Before he fired up his stanky as marijuana, called White Widow, he asked me where my Aunt Pearlie Mae was. I told him she was at work, then he said where

Je'Von and I told him I didn't know. Black sat on the couch and pulled out his bag of cocaine and sprinkled a heavy dose all over the marijuana. He took two snorts of coke up his nose, and then tied the bag back up and rolled his blunts. I shook my head and said, "Hell naw! You ain't smoking that stanky ass shit in here," then I ordered him to go outside on the porch! I got up and walked outside with him so he could smoke his heavy Chevy.

I stood on the other side of the porch because I didn't want to be close to the smoke nor the smell. Before he could finish his dope stick, a dope fiend came up asking for a twenty rock of crack. Black quickly pulled out his sack of rocks and served the crackhead. The crackhead rolled the rock around in his hand a few times while closely examining it, he then quickly handed Black the twenty dollars. A lady walked up and asked for a ten dollar rock. He sold it to her and continued puffin his blunt.

I could see a couple of guys standing on the corner looking our way, mean mugging and looking crazy. One of the guys asked the other guy, "How in the hell this bitch ass nigga think he can just serve on our turf?" I quickly looked in their direction to see who they were referring to because if I heard them, I know Black heard them. I knew some shit would pop off if they were talking about him. Before I could say anything, Black yelled back to the niggas on the corner, "Who the fuck you talking about?"

One of the guys I knew from the hood because he stayed up top in the Georgia Court section of the hood. He tried to down play the situation because he knew me and my brother Je'Von. The other two niggas were still talking mad shit. Black told them that their fake asses needed to move on and quit selling those wolf tickets.

My medication had me feeling good, but I wasn't in the mood for another day of bullshit. Words went back and forth until one of the niggas pulled out . . .

Bong . . . bong . . . bong!

That nigga let loose in our direction. Black ran behind a car and I ran into the house while holding my ribs. As I made my way through the screen door, I heard more gun fire, but at a higher caliber.

Bong . . . bong . . . bong . . . bong . . . bong . . . bong!

I quickly went to my brother's room and raised his mattress and grabbed an M-11 Uzi. I noticed that the clips were double taped together. I checked to see if it was loaded, then I rushed back to the front door.

Pop . . . pop . . . pop . . . pop! Bong . . . bong . . . bong!

I peeped out of the door and Black was bussin' back with them niggas. I went to the back door and ran up the sidewalk until I reached the corner of the project row. I hit the corner and started straying the M-11. Immediately, everybody hit the ground when I started straying. When Black saw that it was me spraying the Mac, he got up from behind the car and stood in the middle of the street bussin' two chrome four nickels. I had emptied the first clip so I pulled, flipped, and then cocked back and went back to dumping.

One of the guys tried to take off running, but Black took aim and hit him in the ass. I watched blood fly out of his ass as he fell to the ground. The other one tried to double back and take off running the other way so I took out behind him, dumping. I quickly stopped because I wasn't in any kind of shape to continue. I was still banged up from the three broken ribs. I stopped, took aim, and squeezed off a three round burst from the Mac. Bong . . . bong . . . bong!

The second guy took two to the leg and side but he kept moving. The guy Black shot with the forty-five was still lying in the street in a pool of blood. I walked over to him, kneeled down and went in his pocket. I took all of his crack and his money. I kicked him in the ass, walked a few feet, picked up his pistol and stuffed it in the waist of my pants. I holla'd, "Black, let's go because someone probably already called the police!" Black spit on the nigga and told him he was lucky he didn't kill his bitch ass.

As I was backing out, I noticed Cookie pulling up. I didn't waste any time getting into the car with Cookie. Black was still in the middle of the street with guns in hand. I rolled the window down and yelled out to Black as I waved for Cookie to pull off. He looked toward my direction, made a dash for his car, and smashed out.

Before we could get four blocks away, we passed four police cars with the lights flashing. I quickly gave Cookie directions of which way to go. I wasn't sure if someone gave the police a description of us or of her car. Lord knows I didn't want to get caught with the Uzi, the drugs, and the gun that I took from the nigga. I didn't want to fuck up my chances of going to college.

I scrolled through my call log and dialed Black's number to see if his crazy ass had made it safely. Cookie got on the highway at Twenty-eighth and Swett's. Before we got on the ramp, I checked the rearview mirror to see if I saw Black's car. Finally he answered the phone and I asked him where he was and if he was aight? He said everything was kosher. I said cool and told him that I'd hit him up later. He agreed and we hung up.

Cookie and I were headed somewhere because she wanted to show me her surprise. We pulled up at an apartment building and entered an apartment. It was nicely decorated with a lot of American and Oriental furniture. I looked around the apartment then asked her, "Whose place is this?"

She said, "It's the surprise that I wanted to show you."

I asked, "This is your apartment?"

She smiled while nodding and said, "This is OUR apartment."

I looked at her and questioned, "Ours?" She said yes and asked me if I liked it. I said let's go try the bed out and we headed straight to the bedroom, got undressed, and headed to the shower.

In the shower, I lathered up the wash ball with body wash and started washing Cookie's body. After I finished with her, she returned the favor. The hot water felt good on my skin along with the body wash. She made sure she paid extra attention to my dick and balls. I got so hard that I was standing at full attention. Once she got all the soap off of my body, she took me into her mouth. I watched her lick around the head and up and down the sides until she got to my balls. She sucked on them for a few minutes, and then she licked back to the head and started sucking me with passion. She went around the head of my dick with her tongue, slow and seductively. She then sped up and sucked on the head while stroking it with her hand. I couldn't take any longer so I grabbed her by the hair and held her head while I fucked her pretty little mouth. She couldn't take all of me in her mouth. I watched her choke and gag a few times and it turned me on even more. I decided to stop so we could dry off and take it to the bedroom.

After we dried off, I made her bend over and grab her ankles. I got down on my knees behind her and started licking her asshole until she was dripping wet. Once the pussy was dripping wet like I wanted, I took my two fingers and spread her lips open and stuck my tongue deep inside of her and moved it all around. I sucked on her clit while I fingered her with two fingers. As I sucked her clit, I searched around with my fingers until I found what I was looking for. I rolled my fingers around on her G-spot in the come-to-me motion. I watch her legs start to tremble and shake. Her breathing got louder and I kept sucking, licking, and fingering her until finally she screamed out in pleasure, "Tre, I'm cumming!"

I quickly withdrew my fingers from her creamy pussy and stuck my tongue deep within her. After she came all over my tongue and face, she started licking it off of my face. After she had cleaned the cum off of my face with her tongue, I was ready to fuck.

Before I went inside of her, she told me to hold on for a moment. She went into the dresser drawer and gave me a small clear device. I asked her what it was and how to use it. She smiled and told me to put it in her ass. I asked her if she was sure and she said yes. I rubbed it up and down her pussy to lube it up, and then I carefully inserted it into her ass. She laid back with her leg spread wide open. I climbed on top, lifted her legs up on my shoulders, and went inside of her. As I entered her, I listened to her suck air into her mouth.

I was harder than steel and I took no time going to work. I slowly stroked the pussy until all of me disappeared inside of her. She closed her eyes and clenched her teeth together while I continued to beat her pussy up. I could feel her muscles tightly wrapped around my dick and it felt good. I slowed up and long dicked the pussy a few times and watched her eyes roll to the back of her head. She started to shake uncontrollably. I watched her breathing and it looked as if her heart was going to pop out of her chest.

Once the shaking stopped and her eyes were opened again, I told her to turn around to the back. I pulled the butt plug out of her ass and I gently eased myself in as far as I could go before she ordered me to stop. I moved at a turtle pace until her ass was wet enough for me to go deeper and faster. Five minutes later, I had a nice rhythm going, but carefully so I wouldn't hurt her. Her ass was hot and tight. I had to fight to stop from busting off. As I closed my eyes and kept stroking, I continued to hold back on my nut. I wanted to flood her ass with my load so I squeezed a little harder to prolong my nut.

Right when I couldn't hold it any longer, I felt her cum running down my leg. I looked down and the cum was gushing out of her pussy. It was pouring out and I could see her pussy opening and closing. As I watched her pussy pulsate, I lost control and came deep into her ass. I tilted my head back and closed my eyes as I shot my load. She took over and started throwing her back at me. My dick had started to feel really sensitive so I pulled out of her and fell straight to the bed with a big smile on my face.

I lad there and caught my breath for a minute, then we got up to take another shower together. I was exhausted so I let her wash me up again. Ten minutes later, we were in bed, fast asleep.

Three hours later, I was awakened by the vibration of my cellphone. I looked at the number and quickly answered it because it was my brother. He had a fit as soon as I answered. I told him to chill and I would bring his Mac-11 to him A.S.A.P.

I woke Cookie up and asked her for the keys to her Avalon and she gladly gave them to me. I kissed her on the forehead and left. As I drove to meet Je'Von, I started thinking about how I was going to pay for college. As I thought about that, I remembered that Diamond's photo was still in my email inbox. I pulled the photo upon the screen and it was the person that I needed it to be.

I arrived at Swett's Plaza and I spotted Je'Von's box Chevy sitting in the parking lot. I pulled up and tilted my head back making a 'what's up' motion. He waved for me to get in the car so I turned the car off and got in the car with him. I gave him the Mac-11 and told him to put my gun up as well. He wasted no time asking me where you get this from? I just smiled and told him what happened earlier. Just then, I remembered the crack that I had taken off dude. I gave it to him and asked him to sell it for me.

Je'Von said cool and I handed him the package. I asked him how much I would make. He looked at it confirmed at least twelve hundred, minimum. I was cool with that because I would then have enough to buy another car. I gave my brother some dap, then quickly jumped back into Cookie's Toyota Avalon and pulled off. I was glad Je'Von didn't ask me about Diamond and that Eric nigga because I was still putting the pieces of the puzzle together.

I called Cookie to let her know that I was on my way back to the crib. She asked me if I was hungry and I responded with a yes. She said she would cook a meal and it would be ready by the time I arrived. I hung up and jumped on the Twenty-eight Exit and quickly got off on Metro Center. I went through two red lights and turned on Buchannan Street. I stopped at T&T Mobile Phone Shop and Carwash. I walked in and a thick brown skinned girl named Priscilla was behind the counter, bad-mouthing some nigga. I bought an extra cigarette lighter, phone charger, and a pre-paid phone card for my Go Phone.

As I was waiting on Priscilla to ring up my purchases and give me my change, I bumped into Lil Jimmy. I called out his name and he turned to see who I was. I quickly said, "What's up Jimmy, long time no see?" He responded, "You Je'Von's lil brother, right?" I said, "Yeah. How you remember?"

Lil Jimmy responded, "You know I don't ever forget a face." I asked him what he had been up to and he told me he's been pushing the cell phones and the car wash thang. I thought to myself, "Shid, you a legend, man." I've heard stories about Lil Jimmy and the Brick Boy Mafia Crew. As I was thinking that to myself, I heard Jimmy say, "You know I got the new book from Mr. Mafia called *Hunting Season?*"

I said, "Oh yeah, what they selling for? My cousin Day Day was telling me about a Mr. Mafia book called *Blueprint of a Hustler.*"

Jimmy said, "Yeah that was his first book then he released a second one called "Brick *Boy Mafia:* The *Heat of the Streets*", and then he dropped *For the Taste of Sex* and now this new one, *Hunting Season.*" I told him to give me a copy of the new one and *Taste of Sex.* I gave him thirty dollars for both books, gave him some dap, and I left.

I got right back on the freeway at the MetroCenter area and headed over to Donaldson Pike. As I pulled up to Cookie's apartment complex, I made sure no one was following me and then I quickly walked up to her apartment door. When I opened the door, I could smell the aroma of the food. I walked into the kitchen to see what Cookie was preparing. The food looked like it was going to be nasty tasting. I asked her what she had made and she said it was a Korean meal. I didn't want to be rude, so I decided to try it. I prayed like hell it didn't taste like it looked. When I bit into it, to my surprise it was delicious.

I went to the bathroom and washed my hands, came back, sat down, and ate. After dinner, I helped Cookie with the dishes then I got on the computer and checked my email. I had no emails but the photo of Diamond. I stared at the screen for a long time, and then I closed it. I thought to myself about how I will be paying Ms. Diamond a visit real soon.

As I finished that order of business, I logged on to Africa Motors' website and started used car browsing. I looked through photos of cars that were within my budget of five thousand and under. I came upon a clean Delta 88 that was priced for thirty-five hundred. I decided that I would go over and look at it as soon as possible, which would be any day now considering I wasn't working. I wrote down the address to Africa Motors and then filled out some job applications online at different companies. I filled out seven applications for companies such as: Coca Cola, Nissan, Verizon, Home Depot, Lowes, The Marriott Hotel and The Double Tree Hotel. After that, I checked my Facebook page and Twitter account. Cookie came in and asked me to watch a movie with her so I logged off.

Chapter 4

A COUPLE OF CRACKHEADS screamed out, "Je'von, Je'von serve me for this seven dollars!" I told them to fuck that, bring me ten or better cause I can't serve no damn seven dollars. Just as the crackheads walked away pissed off, the rain came from out of nowhere. I decided to sit in my Chevy and catch some sells. I fired up a blunt and listened to the rain pound on the roof and hood of the car. It didn't take me long to get tired of that, so I quickly turned on the sound system and let my four-twelves thump. I smoked my blunt, while listening to Lil Wayne talk about how soft his leather is.

Before I knew it, I was bobbing my head and singing with Lil Wayne, *"My leather so soft, my top so soft, these niggas so soft, I probably have it off and I go so hard, I go so hard. I get money—fuck what you talkin bout—straight out the slaughterhouse, straight out the dragon's mouth—fire you can't put out—the rims is poking out."* Just as I was enjoying my blunt and the music, a fiend came up to my car and I cracked the window to see what he wanted to buy. He said he had a fifty. He gave me the balled up money. I slowly took my time unballing it to make sure it was fifty. I gave him two lil rocks and a big one. He looked at it and rushed off. I thought to myself, it is pouring down raining and these fiends don't give a fuck. They will do whatever it takes to get their hit. I smiled to myself and went back to puffing my blunt.

When I turned my music back up, it was Jeezy, so I started back bobbing my head. *"Hypnotize you are hypnotized—hypnotize you are hypnotized, now I comand you niggas to get money, I comand you niggas to get money, I comand you niggas to get money."* I yelled out, "Get money nigga!" Just then, lightning struck and all of the street lights went out.

It scared the shit out of me so I instantly grabbed my glock and started looking around. The rain was pouring down so hard, it was difficult to see out of the front or side windows of my car. I didn't want to be no sitting duck, so I turned the ignition on, hit my headlights and pulled off.

I bust a few blocks and noticed that the power was knocked out throughout the city or at least in this area. I quickly got an extremely good idea after I past a new construction site. I turned around and pulled over at the construction site, I jumped out and grabbed the biggest brick that I could find and put it in my trunk. I drove back to the hood and got the bolt cutters. After I had the bolt cutters and a pair of gloves, I rode over to Charlotte Pike and hoped to myself that the power was out in that area as well. Just my luck, the power was out there also.

I scanned the area for police and passing cars. I didn't see anyone so I quickly pulled into the parking lot, made a U-turn, and then backed up to the door. I popped the trunk, jumped out and grabbed the big bolt cutters, and went to work on the lock. Once I got the lock cut completely off the door, I slid the gate back as far as it would go. I put the bolt cutters back into the trunk and got the brick out. I lifted it up over my head and smashed the window. I started knocking the remaining glass away so I wouldn't get cut by the broken glass. I ran up into the store and broke all of the glass cases that were sitting before me. Once the cases were smashed, I grabbed all of the hand guns that were in all of the cases and ran back to my car. I dropped them into the trunk and ran back into the store. I started grabbing rifles and assault weapons. I hauled ass up out of there and started heading back over to the hood so I could stash the guns. Once the power gets restored and the alarm starts going off, I'd be long gone. I took my time going down Charlotte Pike until I got over by Cohn Adult learning Center and McDonalds, then I took the back route over to Thirty-ninth and Clifton. One I arrived at the stash house; I quickly unloaded the guns and took off to mom's house to get a flashlight. Upon arriving there, I checked on Mom's to see what was going on with her.

After I found out she was alright, I asked her where the spare flashlight was. She said she only had one and I took off back to the stash house.

Since I didn't have a flashlight, I stashed the guns in the floor and went back to the projects to find a crackhead. The first crackhead I saw, I told him that I had a twenty roc for a flashlight. One of the crackheads rushed off to get me a flashlight. When he returned, he had a flashlight but no batteries. I slapped the shit out of him and told him to get the fuck on. He asked me what about his twenty dollars so I pulled my gun and cocked it on him. Finally, he got the message and he didn't waste no time running away from me as fast as he could.

I went back to my mom's house and borrowed four of her batteries for the flashlight. I quickly put the Energizer batteries into the flashlight and hit the switch. I was happy that the flashlight worked. I went back to the stash house and pulled the guns out of the floor. I wanted to know just what I was working with. I laid the guns out and started counting them first. I had a total of forty hand guns and twelve assault and hunting rifles. I pushed all of the revolvers to one side and all of the semi-autos to the other side. I had a 38 Special Snob nose, two 357 Magnums, one chrome and one black. One forty-four Bulldog, two forty-four Magnums, and four different twenty-two revolvers. I had guns, all makes and models. I put the Smith & Wessons, Glocks, Colts; Sig Sauer's all together because I knew that I was keeping all of them. I a total of four Glocks, two Glock forties, one Glock 9mm and one Glock forty-five. A gray and silver Sig Sauer 9 mm and one Sig Sauer forty-five automatic and a Desert Eagle pistol pack collection. It had changeable barrels and clips from the 40, 357, 45, and 50 calibers. I had six different twenty-five automatics and one thirty-two automatic. There was also three Colt forty-five with lemon squeezed, one black one, and nickel plated with a pearl handle, one blue steel gray, one Tech-22, and two Tech-9s. The Tech-22 was see through clear plastic with a matching banana clip. The Tech-9 was silver and black with the short nose barrel and the other one was all black with the holes in the barrel.

There were three Macs, one Mac-10, one Mac-11 and one Mac-90. The rest of the guns were Ruger P-89, Ruger-P90, Beretta 9mm, and a couple of Tara 9mms. I decided to keep all the Desert Eagles, Glocks, Macs, Colts, and Sig Sauers. I stashed them in the wall compartment and started checking out the hunting and assault rifles. Out of all the assault rifles, I decided to keep the one AK-47, one Calico, the SKS, and M-16, Mossberg pump with the pistol grip, double barrel-12 gauge, AR-15, AR-30, and a Remington 308. I knew I could sell the rest of the guns to Black Obama or Bud and Ovadue. I stashed everything that I planned to keep back into the floor and locked the house back up.

Since the power was still out, I thought why not go out to Opry Mills and hit the Gucci and Louis Vuitton store and the Nike outlet. I jumped into the car and drove to the interstate ramp by 28th and Swett's. I quickly got on the road toward the airport area. As I got halfway toward that area, I noticed the power wasn't out on that side of town. I drove out to the Opryland area and noticed that everything was running smoothly as clockwork. I detoured and back towards the airport and then headed out West. Once back in West Nashville, I discovered the power was on so I went to my man J Smooth's crib to buy a quarter ounce of purp. Once I got there, I had to wrestle with him for a good price because I refused to pay one fifty for a quarter ounce. We went back and forth on the price until I agreed on a buck twenty-five.

I started to shoot his greedy ass in the face and take his lil funky ass weed, but I decided to let him make it another day because that's my man. I paid for the purp and left. I went straight to the block to see if some sells was jumping off. I had to get my buck twenty-five back. I found me a cigarillo Dutch master cigar in the back of my glove compartment so I quickly put almost half of the quarter ounce in the blunt. Just as I was licking the blunt together and started running the lighter across it to dry it off, I noticed three police cars coming down Fortieth Avenue, so I quickly got the fuck out of Dodge.

Chapter 5

I WENT OVER TO freaky Bianca's house and hid out for the rest of the night or morning, depending on how you looked at it. As soon as I came through the door, she was asking me where da weed at nigga. I asked her, where the pussy at bitch? She told me not to play cause I couldn't handle the pussy.

I quickly said, "Who? You the one be stunting when you around yo girls Tasha and Sheoka. What it do? It's just you and me now."

She responded, "Jay stop playing and fire the blunt up."

I said, "You going to give a nigga some of that pussy or what?"

She said, "I don't know about you because you be running yo mouth too much."

"You full of shit, but it's cool because I don't want none of your stanky pussy anyway."

Bianca jumped up screaming, "Stanky pussy? My pussy don't stink! My pussy don't stink, nigga," as she stuck her hand down into her shorts and then ran her finger across her nose! Then she ran up on me, "Nigga, smell it!"

I grabbed her and started wrestling with her while saying, "Naw, I don't want to smell that funky shit!" She fought hard trying to get her hands up to my face so I could smell it, but I wouldn't let her arms go free. As we were wrestling, her fat ass was all over me. I got turned on and started squeezing her ass. She fought to break free from my grasp as she was telling me that I better stop before I started something that I couldn't finish.

I got serious and said, "I'm fucking tonight." I asked, "Are you on your period?" She responded, "No, I'm good." I said, "It's on then. Let's get high!" I sparked the blunt up and hit it before I passed it on to her. I ask her, "You ain't been sucking nobody's dick today, have you?"

She responded. "Nigga, you going to make me fuck you up!"

"Yeah right, imagine that," I said. She puffed on the blunt and I sat back and watched her greedy ass keep pulling and pulling. I was thinking to myself, "Gone and smoke up bitch, I'm fucking yo ass all night." She finally passed the blunt back and I hit it a few times, then I heard her say, "Jay, put this X in my ass for me."

I started choking on the blunt. Once I finished coughing, I asked, "What?" She held up the X and repeated what she previously asked. I smiled and said, "Shit, give it to me. She came over and gave it to me and smiled again, then I said pull yo shit down and bend over. She did and I was all smiles. She looked back at me and said damn nigga, what's taking you so long. I told her to hold the fuck up cause I was admiring the view. She told me to admire the view after I put it in her ass. I asked her if she had an X for me. She directed me to get it out of her pocket. I leaned over and searched though her pocket and grabbed a double stack. I put one in her ass and I held on to the other one.

As I pushed the pill into her ass, I told her she better not get no shit on my finger. She peeped back at me and told me to quit fucking playing and put the pill deep into her ass. I pushed it a little deeper and then pulled my finger out. I told her to go get me a glass of water so I could take mine. She said it would be better if I just let her put one in my ass because it dissolves faster. I responded, "Bitch, fuck that! You ain't touching my ass!" She said I was a pussy and I told her to watch her fucking mouth before she finds herself leaking in this motherfucker and then pulled my gun out. She wasn't fazed by my gun, she said, "I hope your dick is as big as your gun." I ordered her to go get the water. As she went to get the water, she looked back over her shoulder and asked if I wanted water or orange juice. I said juice, it's better than water.

As she went to the kitchen, I got out a Viagra and swallowed it without water. I mumbled to myself, "Shit, she think she about to work me on that X and talk shit about it later, well I got a trick for her ass." As the Viagra slowly eased its way down my throat, she returned with the oranges juice. I held up the double stack and popped it into my mouth and gulped the orange juice. As soon as I killed the entire glass of orange juice, I went right back to puffing on my purp. She reached out for the blunt as I passed it to her and I just sat there and stared at her pussy print through her boy shorts.

As she reached out for the blunt again, I grabbed her arm and pulled her over to me and sat her down on my hard dick. I told her to open her mouth, and then I pulled hard on the blunt and gave her a shot gun with the smoke of the blunt. As I was pulling back, I could see her pupils dilating so I knew that she would be rolling and feeling good. As she puffed on the blunt, she started grinding on my dick and I got even harder. I was trying to give myself some time for the Viagra to kick in, but between me smoking the purp and the double stack in my system, I was already too horny.

She passed the roach back to me and unzipped my pants and pulled me out. I instantly popped up out of my zipper like a King Cobra. She said, "Ooooo Jay!" She started jacking my dick, then she spit on it and started stroking it faster. I laid back on the couch and finished the last of the roach while she kept stroking. She finally realized that her spit wasn't enough lube for what she was doing so she put me deep into her mouth. I put the roach out on her back and grabbed her hair and pushed her head all the way down on my dick. She had no problem deep throating my entire dick. I watched in amazement as she went from the tip of my head all the way down to my balls.

I spoke in a low whisper, "Yeah, eat that dick bitch." As she continued to deep throat me, I started coming out of my shirt and wife beater. I was high and feeling good. She gave me head like it was the last supper. I closed my eyes and laid back on the couch as she continued to chew me up. Twenty minutes went by and she was still sucking with fury. I wasn't nowhere close to nutting, so I decided to let her do her thang until she tell me that her neck is tired or something.

My X had kicked all the way in and I was feeling extra freaky. I told her to take off her boy shorts and bring that ass to me. I helped her take off her shorts and True Religon t-shirt, and then I told her to get back on my dick. As she went back to sucking, I turned around and started eating her out while she sucked me off. I wanted to see who would cum first. I stuck my middle finger deep down into her sticky, wet pussy and fingered her for a brief second, and then I pulled out and smelled my finger. The pussy smelled good, so I tasted the pussy off of my finger.

As she continued sucking, I stuck two fingers in her and kept fingering her and she started gyrating her body to my movement. I inserted a third finger into her and kept fingering. Before I knew it, I had my whole hand in her pussy, fisting her. I felt the tension start in my balls and work its way up to the shaft of my dick. I knew that I was about to finally cum as she continued sucking and stroking my dick. The pressure got greater and greater and as the pressure built up in me, I started fisting her pussy faster and faster.

She started moaning and sucking harder and harder. Right about the time I was bussing off deep in her throat, she was cumming all over my hand. I continued to fist her until her pussy started making farting sounds. I then pulled out and looked at my hand. She told me to taste it so I did and it was a lil salty. She grabbed my hand and started licking it until it was completely clean.

I kicked the jeans off of my legs and told her to get on top of me. She got on top of me and started grinding while I was deep inside of her. As she rode me, she started licking my hand again. I leaned into her and started kissing for what seemed like fifteen minutes, then I sucked on her titties as she continued to rock her hips with my hips. I was harder than

Chinese arithmetic as she kept riding and I kept pumping. It took almost an hour and a half for me to get my second nut.

I carried her into the kitchen and put her on top of the washing machine and fucked her for like thirty minutes or so. She was begging me to hit her from the back so I grabbed two pillows off of the couch and placed them underneath my knees, and then I started hitting her doggy-style on the kitchen floor. As soon as I went in doggy-style, she came all over my dick and started whining like a sick dog. I fucked her as hard as I could and she loved every minute of it. She kept begging me to fuck her harder, but any harder than what I was delivering and we would have been joined together like Siamese twins.

I fucked and fucked for another two hours straight, trying to get my third nut, but it just wouldn't come. She started to dry up and the friction was starting to make me chafe from the skin on skin rubbing. I pulled out of her and stared at her swollen red pussy lips. I then started linking her pussy trying to lube her up. She said my pussy is too sore and can't take anymore. I was still chasing my third nut so I said, "Hell naw bitch! You owe me a nut!" She told me to lie down on my back. I asked her, "What you gonna do, ride me again?" She said lay down I got this. With that said, she started licking my asshole and it was feeling so good. I relaxed, laid back and closed my eyes. A few minutes later I could feel the pressure starting to build up deep down in my balls. It started working its way up to my shaft and toward my head.

My mouth was half open and I was breathing hard, anxiously waiting to bust my third nut. Finally, it came! I shot cum out of my dick like a hot volcano spits lava. She devoured all of my fuck juices until she completely drained me dry. When she finished, she asked me, "Are you happy?" I looked at her and I told her, "I love you Bianca."

She responded, "Oh hell no! Get the fuck out of my house with that shit!"

I told her, "Let's cuddle together or go cook me something to eat."

"Nigga, get out. I ain't fucking with you no more," she said. I asked her if I could wash up, but she pointed to the door. I got dressed and left to the rising morning sun. Six hours of non-stop fucking had me walking with a limp.

Chapter 6

As we were watching the movie, the power went out and we sat there wondering what happened. After I realized that it wasn't coming back on no time soon, I told Cookie let's go get some sleep. The next morning, I woke up to the smell of eggs, toast, and sausage. We sat down and at together, and then she had to rush off to work with her mother.

I sat there wondering how I was going to get around looking for a job. I knew I was forced to hit my stash and buy the car from Africa Motors. I decided to call Je'Von to see if he would come and get me. I dialed his number and let it ring. He picked up on the third ring.

"Hey Jay, what's good," I asked?

"Man not shit, just finished fucking freaky Bianca about an hour ago."

I really had no idea who he was talking about, but I was happy for him so I just said, "Was it good?"

He said, "Nigga, she was like an animal!" I started laughing because I started picturing two animal fucking. I quickly got serious and said Jay come scoop me from my lil shawty's house. He said where you at ? I told him off of Harding Place over by the Waffle House. Je'Von said nigga I'm too tired to drive but I'm on my way. I said okay thanks I really appreciate it I'ma buy a new car as soon as you finish that lil situation that I asked you to handle. Je'Von said I'm finished with that and I have the money for ya. I said cool that's what up can you take me to get a new whip? I need to find a new job a.s.a.p. Je'Von didn't think I needed to get a job. He said you better get yo ass in "the game" and stop waiting on them crackers to hire You. I wasn't trying to hear all that so I told him to call me when got to the Harding Place exit and I would be outside waiting for him. He said "cool" and hung up.

Once I finished talking to him, I called the Tennessee Titan headquarters and asked to speak with Diamond. It took five minutes before she finally got on the phone. As soon as I heard the voice, I said, "Hello Ms. Diamond." She said, "Hey, how are you and who am I speaking with?"

I answered, "This is Tre'Von."

"Who, I'm not sure I know you," she said.

"Sure you do. You got me hit over the head, my ribs broken, and my car blown up," I reminded her. She got really quiet for a second and I continued, "Ooh, you remember me now, right?" She quickly asked "why are You calling my job? I said because we had some unfinished business that we need to handle.

"I don't think so. That was only a one-night thang," she said. I laughed and said No sweet heart You are misunderstanding why I'm calling You. We need to discuss what happened and I need to know all of the details about Eric and his friend.

She responded with an attitude, "Please, I'm not getting into all of that. He is not my concern so please don't call here anymore because we have nothing to talk about. Now if you will excuse me, I've got to get back to practice."

I warned her, "Do what you like, but before you go back to practice; you should know that either you talk to me about Eric or you will be talking to Detective Mills."

She was shocked, "What?" I asked her what You think those white folks will say to You when Metro police come down to your job with a warrant to question You about Your involvement in the assault. Before she could speak, I said it's not going to be good for the business and surely it will make the news. She changed her tune real quick and told me to call her later and we could talk. I warned her again by telling her that she better not try to play me or I would make sure her life would be turned upside down by the cops and the news media. She had to go but she told me to call back after five o'clock. I smiled to myself because I knew that I had her full attention. I needed to know who this Eric guy was and she was going to help me whether she liked it or not.

Twenty minutes later, Je'Von called and told me that he was getting off at the Harding Place exit so I gave him the directions to the apartment and started to head out of the door so I could meet him in parking lot. As I headed out of the front door, all of the pictures and windows started rattling so I knew that it was Je'Von with his loud ass music. I rushed out of the door, hurrying to get into the car. I thought to myself, "Why does he always have the damn music so loud?" I walked up to the car, pulled the door handle, and the moment the door opened, the music jumped out at me.

Je'Von nodded his head in the 'what's up' motion and I immediately reached for the radio volume. He looked at me with a crazy look and I told him he couldn't come out here with his loud ass music, especially all early in the morning. He didn't like that and he said, "Nigga, you need to hurry up and get yo own car!" I said today is the day so pay up. He just shook his head and reached in his pocket and counted out a thousand dollars.

I questioned him, "I thought you said I would make at least twelve hundred at a minimum?"

"Slow down greedy ass nigga, I ain't do that shit fo nothing," Je'Von said.

"Oh, it's like that? I thought you was going to help me out," I asked?

"Yeah, I just did, but next time sell yo own cake."

"Man, you know I'm not a drug dealer. I'm trying to go college. Or did you forget that one day I'ma be a lawyer, if not that, a Metro police officer?"

Je'Von was agitated, "What, a policeman? I should shoot yo dumb ass right now for saying that dumb ass shit. Why you want to be a stanky ass pig Tre? What you need to be doing is trying to get yo money and stop bullshitting around. We can take over these streets. We can be just like those Brick Boy Mafia niggas, you and me, Tre. You heard me? You and me . . . you watch my back and I'll watch yours. Either niggas get money with us or we blow shit up! You feel me Tre? Huh, you feel me?"

I said, "Man, you sound stupid bro. There ain't no future in that drug shit so you better get out before you can't get out. I know what I'ma do and what I'ma do is take my black ass to college so I can bust wild brothers like you."

Je'Von went ballistic, "So what you saying nigga? You gonna bust me? Huh, you gonna bust me Tre? Your own fucking brother! That's crazy and I'm telling Momma. See what you need to do is bust that motherfucker who busted yo head open and broke your ribs! Yeah Tre, whatever happened with that? Huh Tre? Why you didn't bust his ass? Why Tre, why? Why haven't you shot his ass, bust him! Bust him, Tre! Here, you can use my gun!"

I told Je'Von to put that damn gun away before them white folks call the police on us and we both go to jail. Jay said fuck them crackers, I'm not getting a job and I don't give a fuck about no jail. He said, "I'ma hold court in the street, nigga and then run, nigga. I'll let you deal with the cops!"

"Man, will you pull off so I can go get my money and buy me a new car? It's too early in the morning to be going back and forth with your dumb ass. And since you asked, I got in touch with Diamond and I going to meet with her later so we can discuss that Eric nigga that blew up my car."

"That's what I'ma talking about! It's finally time to blow some shit up," Je'Von said! "What do you mean you gonna meet her later? Shit, nigga I'm going with you and after we get the info that we want, I'ma put her ass in the trunk!"

"I said just chill, man. Why you always got to be negative? Just sit back and let me handle it my way, the smart way without the gun play."

Je'Von protested, "Man fuck what you talking about, that bitch gonna get it if she ain't talking right. No ifs, ands, buts, or maybes about it. Somebody ass gots to pay and that's the end of the fucking discussion.

(Music blasting)

"My glocks spitting rounds, niggas falling down clutching their stomach, its west side death Row, thug niggas on the rise must've shot me five times real niggas don't die, can you feel me laced with game, I know you feel me. You can say what you want but cowards fear me. My only fear of death is reincarnation, heart of soldier with the brain to teach the whole nation. Screaming no mo pain, I can bring the pain, hardcore from the brain. Let's step inside my astroplane, nigga I came to bring the pain, hardcore from the brain."

We rode in silence the whole ride over to Mom's house. I was deep in thought and I knew Je'Von was listening to that loud music. As we pulled up at Mom's, I was surprised to see that she was home. I should ask her why in the world she ever messed around with Je'Von's daddy because his ass is crazy so I know it had to be passed down from his daddy because my Momma didn't act like that. I was glad we had different dads because the world wasn't ready for two lunatics like Je'Von, one is enough. I got out of the car and walked into the house and gave her a hug.

We talked for a while and I was happy to know that Mom's was healthy and feeling good. It saddened me that she had to work so hard just to pay bills and to try to get ahead. I swore to myself that I would try to find a good job so I can help her with the bills. I knew she was pushing close to forty-five years old and I didn't want her living in the projects all of her life. I wished my drunk ass daddy had chosen us over his bottle of alcohol, but it is what it is, can't turn back the hands of time. He had his faults and he made his choice.

At least he didn't go out like Je'Von's daddy, a drug addicted fool that beat women to support his drug habit. It's crazy that he was so strung out on drugs that he used to buy from his own son. Maybe that's why

Je'Von is so fucked up in the head considering he's the one who sold him the dope that killed him. I remember reading the newspaper just like it was yesterday, *Man Found Dead from Overdose.* He had so many drugs in his system that his heart exploded in his chest and his lunges collapsed. When the police found him, he still had the needle in his arm and a crack pipe in his pocket. The detective came to the house and gave Momma the news and she was devastated. Je'Von made me promise not to ever say a word about him supplying the drugs to his dad. If Momma knew what I knew, she'd probably have a nervous breakdown.

I snapped out of my thoughts as she called my name for the third time. I looked around until my eyes met with hers and I answered, "Yeah Ma, what is it?"

She responded, "Boy, are you okay?" I've called you three times and I can tell that something deep is on your mind. Is everything alright Tre?"

"Yes ma'am. I was just thinking about this new car that I'm about to purchase. Je'Von is about to take me to pick it up."

Just as she was about to speak, the phone rang. I watched her answer it and heard her say, "Yes. Right now? Okay, no problem, just give me one hour and I'm there." She hung up the phone and I asked her what was going on. Mom explained that she had to go work; they needed her to come in on her day off. Before I could protest, she was already heading to her bedroom to change into her work clothes. I cursed myself because at this rate, my mom probably wouldn't live to see sixty-five. I knew I had to hurry up and get another job so I could save my money for law school so I could become a lawyer. The only problem was, could Mom hold on for another four to six years of me finishing college and getting hired at a law firm? Becoming a Metro police officer had to be easier and less time to attain. Damn! What am I going to do, I thought to myself? I knew that I had to come up with something quick.

As Moms rushed out the door, Je'von came in screaming and cursing, Momma told him to watch his damn mouth and he just ignored her like she hadn't spoken a word. Finally, I asked him if he was ready to take me over to Africa Motors. He said not really, but let's go because the sales were booming out there. He said he needed more coke. I just shook my head, thinking to myself, what all those niggas going to do when I become the police and I clean-up this neighborhood? I wanted my neighborhood to be safe for good people like my momma. I didn't want her living like this and I especially didn't plan to let my unborn kids live in this environment.

As Je'Von kept screaming, "Tre bring yo ass on or I'ma leave yo monkey ass!" That snapped me out of my thoughts and I went to my room to get my stash out of my shoe box. There was only thirty-five hundred dollars in the shoe box plus the grand that Je'Von gave me for the crack, made forty-five hundred. I had to find a dependable car, but cheaper than forty-five hundred. I grabbed the money and hurried out of the front door and into Je'Von's car. He pulled away like a bat out of hell. I asked Je'Von what was the hurry and he said he had to re-up. He said money is everywhere and I got to get back to it.

It only took us twenty minutes to get to the car lot. I told Je'Von to help me find something worth buying for my money. He wanted me to get a lot of shit that I couldn't afford. I looked at Dodge Chargers, Magnums, and Chrysler 300s. I came up on a 1982 Chevy Nova for fifteen hundred so I asked to test drive it. We took it around the block and it drove real good, but it was a lil small for considering I'm six foot tall. We pulled back into the lot and I told the salesman that I needed something for around the same price, but larger. The salesman showed me a 1988 Chevy Suburban that had just been re-poed. I lifted the hood and everything under it was fairly new. The guy told me the owner went to jail for dog fighting and he used to haul dogs around in the truck so they had to repo it once he was incarcerated.

I asked how much and the guy said the price was three thousand cash or a grand down to take over the note that was abandoned by the guy that got locked up. I counted out three thousand and told him to get the paperwork started. The paperwork was completed and signed in less than twenty minutes. I was the proud owner of new vehicle. My only problem now would be affording gas in this bad economy.

I told Je'Von to meet me back at mom's house. I jumped in my new truck and headed back to West Nashville. I turned on the radio to hear how it sounded.

(Music flowing from the speakers)

Cause I may be bad, but I'm perfectly good at it. Sex in the air, I don't care cause I like the smell of it. Sticks and stones may break my bones but chain and whips excite me. So come on, come on. So come on, come on, come on. See, I may be bad, but I'm perfectly good at it. Sex in the air, I don't care cause I like the smell of it.

I rocked my head to the music and yelled out to myself, "Okay, sing it Rihanna, you go girl!" I listened to that song and then Keri Hilson's song, "Pretty Girl Rock," came on. I pulled over and filled the truck up and proceeded back to my mom's house to put the money back in the box. Once I arrived, I put what was left of my money away and sat down on the couch. I sat there thinking for a long while. No one was calling me back about a job and the clock was ticking for me if I was going to enroll in college at the University of Miami. I made my mind up that if no one called me by next week, then I was going back to stripping. I had to do something if I was going to be successful and get Mom out of the projects.

Chapter 7

I WAS SO DEEP in thought that I forgot about calling Diamond back after five o'clock. I looked at my watch and it was already seven o'clock. I decided to go pay her visit and see what the business was. I got up off of the couch and headed for the 'burban. As I got behind the wheel, I thought about it and decided that I shouldn't go alone. As much as I hated the idea, I really had no choice, so I texted Je'Von and I told him I needed him to go with me to Diamond's house. He texted me right back. His text said he'd be there in five minutes.

I sat in the truck waiting on him to pull up. A few minutes later, he pulled in behind me. I watched him from my rearview mirror. I saw him stuff a gun down his pants, and then he got out of his car and walked toward mine. When he got into the truck, he didn't waste no time saying, "I got the strap. Let's go and make this bitch talk!"

I put the 'burban in drive and pressed the gas pedal. I turned to my brother and said, "Look Jay, we are just going to talk to her. Don't get on no crazy shit." He said if the bitch didn't talk, he was going to make her talk. I told him to stop being negative and violent all of the time. I asked him to chill out just this one time and let me handle the situation my way.

"Fuck that Tre; you can't be all soft with this bitch! You got to let her know that you ain't playing no games with her stank ass!"

I tried to calm him down, "Chill Jay. She cool, we just going to sit down and talk it out."

Jay responded, "Talk? Shit nigga, she betta be talking motherfucking right or I got something that will make her talk loud and clear!"

We wasn't even out of the projects yet and I already started to regret the situation. Damn, why didn't I just call Black to come with me? At least he's a bit more civilized.

The traffic was clear on the freeway, so we got to her apartment faster than I expected. I started to get butterflies in my stomach. I didn't want to appear nervous so I tried to play it cool, be more like Je'Von than myself. As we approached the gate, I thought to myself, how are we going to get through the gate without the code?

I flipped out my Samsung Note and dialed up her number. It took her three rings to answer, but she finally answered. I told her I was outside the apartment gate and she needed to buzz me through or give me the code to open it. She seemed to be pissed that I had come over instead of calling, but I really didn't give a fuck. Just as I thought she was going to say something slick, a car passed us to enter through the gate. I nearly tore the axle off of the 'burban, speeding behind the entering car before the gate closed.

She was still on the phone telling me that I should have done this or that as we were pulling up to her apartment. I waved to Jay and we got out and started walking to her door. She was still talking about nothing as we knocked on the door. I guess she wasn't thinking, but she told me to hang on because someone was at her door. I listened to her walk through the apartment toward the front door. As she opened the door, I smiled and said, "Hey beautiful, it's me." She hung the phone up and I asked her if we could come inside. Before she even had a chance to answer, I pushed by her and Je'Von followed.

I could see the fire in her eyes. She quickly said, "I didn't say you could come in and who is he?

"You didn't say 'no' either and he's my brother," I responded.

She questioned. "Why you bring him?"

"To prevent me from getting jumped again. Why you think," I asked?

"You act like I had something to do with that. I helped you, remember?"

"Yeah, I remember, so help me again and then I'm out of your hair for good," I said.

Diamond responded, "I don't know about that. I think I'ma mind my own business because after all, I didn't mess with Eric like that so that's between you two." I told her it was cool if she didn't want to get involved and all I wanted to know was where he lived, where he hung out, and what nickname people called him in the streets. She was determined not get involved and she asked why she should give me that information. I quickly told her that I didn't want to put the police into her business and make shit bad for her at work.

She responded, "See, that's what I been thinking about. It's been over a month since that shit happened, so I don't really think you got a case. After all, it's my word against your word that I even know you or that you were even ever over her. So, why would I help you? What do I get out of it?"

Before I could speak, Je'Von began answering her questions, "Well for starters bitch, you get to keep yo life! Is that enough?" Diamond jumped up like she wanted to fight, so Je'Von immediately pulled the Mac out of his pants and told her to sit down. He said, "Bitch, I knew you were gonna be on some bullshit!"

I tried to calm Jay down, "Jay, just chill man and put that gun away. It's no need for us to go there."

Jay didn't seem to hear me as he became more aggressive, "Naw, fuck that and fuck this bitch! She gonna talk or I'ma spill this bitch's guts!" I tried even harder to diffuse the situation by telling Je'Von to chill out and to stop tripping. He continued to ignore me. He asked Diamond, "So what's it gonna be, bitch?"

Diamond was cocky, she said, "You won't shoot me cause my neighbors will hear the gunshot and someone will call the police and both of you dumb ass niggas will go to jail." She jumped up to run toward her cordless phone. I jumped up to block her cause I didn't want shit to happen like this. As I blocked her path, I quickly wrestled the phone out of her hand and then I heard Je'Von cock the Mac. Diamond and I stopped and turned to see what was going on and Je'Von was pointing the gun in our direction but at her.

Diamond mumbled in a low voice, "Do it, come on do it. I dare you!" Je'Von shot the gun at the couch and feathers flew everywhere. By the look on her face, she was beginning to realize that the gun wouldn't make a sound if Je'Von chose to shoot again. He ordered her to sit down. He told her the next one was going through her skull. Diamond sat down and he ordered me to tie her up. I told him I wasn't going to do that. Je'Von had checked out and he even told me he wasn't playing with me.

I saw the look in his eyes, so I quickly started looking for something to gag her with. As I searched for an extension cord or tape, I was careful not to touch anything with my bare hands. The whole time I was thinking that this situation didn't have go down like this. I found clear packing tape. I grabbed it and ran back to the living room. I taped her mouth, being careful not to tape over her nose so she could breathe and then I taped her hands behind her back.

Je'Von stood in front of Diamond and kneeled down to be face to face with her. I heard him tell her, "Listen bitch, I'ma ask you some questions and You betta get the answer right if you know what's good for you." Diamond mumbled through the tape. Je'Von told her don't try to speak, but to nod her head. After he finished telling her that, he told me to sit and be quiet.

Je'Von asked, "Do you know Eric's last name?" Diamond nodded yes. "Do you know where he lives?" She nodded yes. Then he asked, "Do you know where he hangs out at?" She nodded yes and no. Je'Von said, "Okay, we'll come back to that question. Who is the nigga that was with him?" She looked, but didn't say anything, so Je'Von asked, "Do you know him?" She nodded yes. Je'Von asked one last question, "Do you want to help us find him" She was silent for a moment then she finally nodded yes.

Diamond looked up at me with tears in her eyes as if to say, 'please help me, your brother is crazy,' but all I could do was look away. I felt bad for her, but it was too late to go against Je'Von. He ordered me to stand her up on her feet because she was going with us. We walked to the front door and Je'Von peeped out first and I held onto Diamond. He gave me the go ahead and we all quickly walked out of the apartment and headed to the truck. He put her in the back seat and we both got up front. Je'Von told me to drive. We took off toward the entrance of the complex, as we approached the gate it automatically opened and we turned out onto the street.

Je'Von reached back over the seat and snatched the tape off of Diamond's mouth. She instantly hollered and started rubbing her mouth on the side of her shoulder. Je'Von asked her where Eric hung out. She got quiet so he told Diamond that he wasn't going to play around with her and he was only going to ask one time. Diamond responded, "He lives in Antioch, off of Blue Hole Road."

Je'Von asked, "What kind of car does he drive? What's his last name and where does hang?" Diamond said he had several cars but he mostly drives a Dodge Charger. "What color and what else does he drive" Je'Von asked? She said the Charger was black. He drives a white Mercedes with white wheels, and a black Escalade with black wheels.

Je'Von ordered me to drive to Blue Hole Road so we could find the clown Eric. He asked Diamond for Eric's last name and the name of the dude that was with him. She said Eric's last name was Johnson and the other guy was Shawn Brown. Je'Von asked her again, "Now where you say he lives?" She responded, He lives in Brentwood off of Concord road."

Je'Von responded, "First you said he lived off of Blue Hole Road?"

"No, he be hanging on Blue Hole Road with Shawn."

When Je'Von asked her what Eric did for a living, she got quiet. I looked over the back seat and she finally responded that he sells drugs. Je'Von asked her where he sold his drugs and where he kept his drugs. Diamond said she didn't know any of that. Je'Von asked her what color panties she had on and Diamond responded with a 'what.' Je'Von told her to stay focused and tell him where Eric kept his dope.

Diamond revealed, "He has a warehouse storage off of the intersection of Bell Road and Nolensville Road, going toward Brentwood." Je'Von said I need You to show me the house off of Blue Hole Road, the warehouse storage where he keep his drugs, and the house out in Brentwood.

Once we were coming down Blue Hole Road, Diamond told me to turn onto Sue Court. We kept driving until we reached Sue Court. Diamond told me to go all the way down to a brown brick house. As we rolled up to the house, she nodded her head toward the house.

Je'Von asked Diamond, "Are you sure this is the house?"

Diamond responded, "Yes, I'm sure."

He said, "Okay bitch, let's see how sure you are. Do he have cameras around the house?"

"I'm not sure, but I think so," Diamond stated.

"Do he have an alarm system or dogs?"

"I don't know about an alarm system, but he does have dogs," Diamond informed.

Je'Von said he had an idea, he jumped out of the truck and opened the back door and waved for Diamond to get out. I asked him what the fuck he was doing. He said to follow his lead and have my gun ready just in case the nigga shows his face. He snatched Diamond up by the shirt, telling her to hurry up. Je'Von march her ass right up to the front door and rung the doorbell. He told her if he answers, tell him Eric sent you.

Je'Von ordered me to stand on the side of the house and to keep an eye out for the back door and the other eye on anything that might not look right. He made Diamond ring the doorbell again. When no one answered, Je'Von grabbed Diamond by the neck and marched her to the side of the house where I was standing. I asked Je'Von, "What now?"

He said, "Let's try the back door. It's looking like nobody is here."

Just then, dogs started barking and Je'Von pushed Diamond toward me and told me to watch her as he took off toward the chain link fence. When Je'Von got to the fence, he quickly scanned the backyard for cameras. He didn't see any cameras so aimed for the two chained up pit bulls, he squeezed the trigger and dropped the two dogs without making a sound and then he hopped the fence with a single leap. Diamond and I watched as he went to the backdoor and turned the knob, but it was locked. Je'Von stepped back and kicked the door. On the third kick, the hinge broke and the frame split.

I ran to Je'Von and warned him, "Jay, what the fuck? That shit was loud as fuck and man we need to go right now!" He told me to chill out and bring Diamond. He finished ramming the door in with his shoulder which caused him to fall into the house on the kitchen floor. He leaped back up to his feet, pointing the gun at nothing but air. He waved for me to bring Diamond inside as he ran back to the truck to get the tape. He came back in the house, tore a piece of the tape off with his teeth and firmly placed it across Diamond's mouth. He also taped her feet so she wouldn't be able to get away.

Je'Von ordered me to help him look around. I stood there for a moment, but I started to look around to see what I could find. I started looking in the living room and Je'Von ransacked the kitchen, I heard him say out loud to himself, "I need to slow down. Where would I hide my shit if I had something hide?"

Then I heard him say out loud again, "Shit, I know just the place to look!" He went straight to the refrigerator, freezer, and into the deep freezer.

I removed all of the meat from the deep freezer until I got close to the bottom and then there it was, "Bingo! That nigga thought he was slick!" I pulled up four saran wrapped blocks of cash money. I instantly told Tre to get in here. He came running, looking scared as shit. I showed him the money and his eyes damn near popped out of his head. I gave him the money and told him to help me look for more. I went to the pantry, looking for more cash. All I found was a Cummins money counter so I grabbed that and sat it on the kitchen table with the four packages of money.

I looked into the oven and in the cabinets. I saw the cereal boxes; I picked one and looked in it. "Bingo!" I found stacks of money with rubber bands around them. There were eight boxes of cereal, but only six of the boxes had money in it and the other two were really cereal. I threw the money on the table with the rest of the loot.

I took off upstairs to check the bathroom and the bedrooms. I checked the dirty clothes hamper in the bathroom and came up with nothing, so I moved on. I looked through the cabinets under the sink and came up empty handed. Something told me to check the shower and medicine cabinet so I did. There was nothing in the shower so I moved on to the medicine cabinet. All was cool as I looked through it but when I tried to shut it, I could tell something was off. I stared at it for a moment and then I went to see if I could lift it off of the wall. To my surprise, it fell halfway and I started fucking with it. It wouldn't lift up, but it pulled up and out of the wall to reveal a hole in the wall. I leaned up against the sink and stuck my arm in and realized that something was in there. I stuck both hands in and pulled whatever it was up and out of the wall. When I finally got it out, I knew right away what it was. I smiled and said to myself, "Oh yeah, jackpot! You slick motherfucker you, I got yo ass now!"

I sat the dope on the counter and stared at it. As I was about to head to the bedroom, I heard Tre'von calling out for me. I quickly ran to see what he found. He had flipped the mattresses and there were six guns lying under there. I told Tre to grab all of them and let's keep looking through the rest of the bedrooms. As he scooped up the guns, we both noticed headlights pull into the driveway. I peeped through the blinds and told Tre, "We got company."

I could see the fear in Tre's eyes so I told him, "Don't worry, we got this nigga. Let's get downstairs before he enters the door." We quickly ran down the stairs and waited as we heard the key in the door starting to turn. I stood behind the door and waited with the strap pointed where his head would probably be, depending on how tall he might be.

Finally the door opened and he stepped in and closed it behind him. As he reached for the light in the living room, I put the strap to his head and said, "You move, you die, nigga" He put his hands up and asked me what I wanted.

I slapped him with the pistol and told him, "Shut up, bitch! I ask all of the questions." Tre came from the kitchen and I told him to search him. Tre patted him down and pulled a 9mm from his waist. I slapped him with the pistol once more across the back of the head and blood flew everywhere as he fell to one knee and grabbed the back of his head.

"Get yo bitch ass up and put yo damn hands up," I ordered. I told Tre'Von to tape his hands behind his back. After he was taped up, I pushed him down onto the couch and asked him for his name. He said his name was Tim Snow and I asked him are You sure about that? I told Tre to stand him up and get his wallet out of his back pocket. He pulled the wallet out and his driver's license read Shawn Brown. I showed him the ID and I said, "Oh yeah, well who is this?"

He looked at it and said it was a fake id with his alias on it. I slapped him with the pistol again and watched blood drip into his eyes until he could no longer see me. I sat him down on the couch and I told him it was his last chance to tell me who he really was. He responded that he had told me once. I instructed Tre to bring Diamond. He brought the bitch in and she immediately started crying when she saw all of the blood on Shawn. I told Tre to wipe the blood out of his face. When he saw Diamond, he was stunned. I smiled and said, "Surprise nigga!" Then I pulled the duct tape off of Diamond's mouth. She hollered from the tape being removed.

I asked Diamond, "Who is this?" She looked at him and then back at me as tears streamed from her eyes and down her pretty little cheeks. She looked back at me and she said, "Shawn." He dropped his head and looked stupid. I kicked him in his chest and he fell out of his seat and onto the floor. Diamond cried harder and I told that bitch to shut up before I get her next.

I stood over the nigga and said, "Listen nigga, Im'a ask you one time. Where yo boy Eric at?" His eyes got big when I mentioned Eric. Shawn responded, "I don't know, dawg. I haven't seen him in over a week. Listen man, I got money, if that's what you want? Just let me go and I'll take you to it."

I smiled and said, "Nigga you broke! I got that money out of the freezer and the cereal boxes. Oh yeah, and the coke or whatever that was in the wall of medicine cabinet, I got that too." Shawn cursed under his breath and looked to the floor. Blood was still leaking from his head onto his shirt and down onto his cream couch. Finally, he spoke, "Listen bro, you got my money. Why don't you just let me go?"

I demanded to know, "Where in the fuck is Eric?" He tried to respond, "Listen bro . . ." I quickly interrupted, "I ain't yo fucking bruh. You see that nigga standing right there with that Uzi," and I pointed to Tre'Von and looked over to him? "That's my bruh! Yo bitch ass homeboy Eric violated him so I'ma violate yo ass." I watched as his bitch ass got all teary eyed on me and then he finally said, "Listen bruh, I mean partner; I don't know your brother. Man, please just take the money and let me go."

I said, "Naw nigga, it ain't that simple. I don't just want your money. I also want yo life. This is yo last chance to live bitch. Where is Eric and tell me about the ware house?"

He stuttered for a brief moment, and then he said, "I swear bruh, I don't know where Eric is and I don't know nothing about a ware house." I said, "Okay, that's yo word," I pulled the pistol up to his eye level and placed it between his eyes and continued, "then I'll see you in hell."

Diamond screamed out, "Wait please!" She began to beg, "Shawn, please tell him what he wants to know. I already told him about the warehouse and Eric's Brentwood house."

"Call Eric up and tell him to come over here so you and him can talk," I demanded.

Shawn responded, "I can't do that. Eric will kill me!"

I gritted my teeth, "Naw nigga! I'll kill you if don't call!"

Shawn shouted, "Well gone and do what you got to do!"

"Okay, tough guy, I got something better in store for you. Tre get the dope, money, and the guns we're going for a ride." Tre'Von ran to the kitchen to get the money, drugs, and the guns. I put two bullets in the forehead of Diamond and watched her body fall to the floor. As I turned back towards Shawn and said, "Oh don't worry tough guy. I got something real special for you." He stared at Diamond's lifeless body and just cried.

Tre'Von ran back into the room with a large garbage bag slung over his shoulder. Tre'Von started to speak, "Jay I got the . . . what the fuck happened? Jay, what did you do? No Jay, no why you shoot her Jay?" I looked at Shawn with a stone face and said, "Let's go. I got plans for this nigga here." Shawn closed his eyes as if he was trying to clear his memory of what he had just witnessed.

"Get the fuck up tough guy, we bout to go on a ride. We gonna see just how tough yo bitch ass really is!" I reached down and snatched Shawn up by the neck with one hand. I turned and told Tre'Von let's go. Tre stared at the dead body of Diamond. "For the last time Tre, let's go!" Tre didn't move so I went over and slapped his face. He snapped out of his trance and I said, "Tre let's go. You got to drive!" As I was exiting with the pistol in Shawn's back, I turned to look at Tre'Von. He was behind me every step of the way, but when he reached the doorway, I saw him turn and look at Diamond's body one last time before he stepped out.

We quickly walked to the truck and pulled off. Tre'Von asked in a low voice, "Yo Jay, where are we going?" I told him we were going out west to 39th.

Shawn spoke, "I should have known you were a Westside nigga, all ya'll are the same."

I responded, "Naw, you are wrong; we ain't all the same. I'm worst than any of them niggas than you ever seen or knew." I told Tre'Von to cut the radio on so I don't have to listen to that bitch ass nigga, he was trying to talk me to death. Tre'Von put a CD in and Boosie Bad Azz roared through the door speakers.

We pulled up on 39th and I quickly took Shawn into the house and sat him down. I told Tre'Von to give me the bag with the drugs, money, guns, and the currency counter in it. After he handed me the bag and I told him to tape Shawn's mouth up so no one would hear his mouth. I quickly put the guns in the floor with the guns from the gun store heist. I put the drugs and money into a different stash and headed back into the living room. I told Tre'Von I needed to make a run so he had to watch Shawn. Tre'Von was okay with that but wanted me to bring him something back to eat. I told him okay and to make sure he keeps his eye on Shawn at all times. I exited the house and jumped into the truck and sped off.

I t took me almost twenty-five minutes to get there but I pulled up at Home Depot and quickly walked in and strolled down the aisle. I grabbed a shopping cart and started putting what I needed in the basket. I grabbed a cordless drill, a cordless saw, two extension cords, a box of razor blades, one utility knife/box cutter, vise grips, wire pliers, one box of nails, a nail gun, rope, and a blow torch. I paid for my items and quickly left heading to Kroger's grocery store to buy the rest of my inventory.

Once I arrived there, I purchased a can of lighter fluid, Idaho potatoes, a jug of anti-freeze coolant, one large box of salt, and some 40 gallon trash bags. I paid cash and headed out the door. As I was rushing to get back, I remember that I had to stop and get Tre'Von something to eat so I got off of the interstate at Trinity Lane and went up to Arby's at the Pilot gas station and truck stop.

I went through the drive thru, got the food, paid and kept it moving. I got back on the interstate at Trinity Lane and headed over to the 28th Avenue exit. I pulled up at the house, went in and gave Tre-Von his food. I left again and went up to Skyview Apartments and gave a crackhead Shirley a half of a gram to use her car. She quickly handed over the keys and I left in a hurry. Once I was back at the house, I told Tre'Von to grab Shawn so we could go. I had to help Tre'Von get Shawn to his feet and forced him out to the trunk of the car.

I stuffed his ass in there and we sped off into the night. I drove for an hour or so without any idea of where I was going. Tre'Von asked me where we were heading and I told him we were going to Joelton. Tre asked what was in Joelton. I told him to sit back, enjoy the ride, and he would see.

Tre'Von suddenly snapped out and said, "How in the fuck am I supposed to enjoy the ride when you got this faggot ass nigga screaming through duct tape and beating on the trunk?"

I Said, "He taped up and it's hot in there. What do you think he gonna do?"

"Well you need to do something with him because I'm tired of riding around with him. What if we get pulled over," Tre'Von asked?

'We are almost there so just chill out." Tre'Von reached for the radio and turned it on. J-Cole poured out of the speakers I continued to drive until I came up on an abandoned warehouse that looked like it was about to far apart. I pulled up to it and jumped out. I ran around to the side of the building and broke the window out. I didn't hear an alarm sound off so I went back to get Tre'Von. I told him to climb through the window of the warehouse and let the door up or unlock the back door, if it had one. A few seconds after I helped him climb through the broken window, he unlocked the door and I smiled.

I walked in and looked around and then I headed back to the trunk of the car to get Shawn out. I forced him into the warehouse and sat him down. I got all of the items that I had purchased from the inside of the car and took them into the warehouse. I slung a rope over the ceiling beam and pulled on it to see just how much pressure it could take. Once I was convinced that it should hold, I told Tre'Von to help me tie Shawn up by his arms. We started tying him up and he started mumbling through the duct tape. After he was secured, I took the utility knife out and inserted a fresh new razor blade into it and cut his shirt off and then his pants and boxers.

Tre'Von wasted no time saying, "Damn bro, what you finna do?" I told him I'm finna make this bitch talk. I said to Shawn, "Listen up bitch, since you so tough, we about to see."

I asked him, "Tell me about the warehouse and the dope?"

Tre'Von reminded me, "Hey Jay, his mouth is still taped up. How he gonna talk?" I told Tre'Von to pull the shit off. He removed the tape and Shawn hollered like a bitch. I asked him again, "Where is the coke and the money?"

Shawn said, "Fuck you nigga, I don't know!"

"Wrong answer," I said. I cut a hole in the bag of Idaho potatoes and grabbed a handful out. I threw them at him for target practice. The brick hard potatoes hit him like a brick and I listened to the blows knock the wind out of him. "Where the dope at?"

"You got it all! It was in my house!"

"Tell me about the warehouse," I asked?

"I don't know nothing about no fucking warehouse," Shawn yelled!

"Okay, maybe this will help you remember," and I grabbed four the biggest potatoes and slung them at him. The first one hit him in the chest, the second one hit him in the face, and the last two hit him in the lower abdomen and in his nuts. His face started to swell instantly and he grunted in pain as the last two potatoes hit his stomach and his nuts. I withdrew a few more potatoes and hurled them at him with deadly force that delivered body and facial blows. I watched as blood started to ooze out of his nose and from the side of his eye as he fought to hold in the pain

I asked again, "Are you ready to tell me about the warehouse?"

He spat blood into my face and said, "Fuck you, nigga!"

I calmly wiped his bloody spit off of my face and walked over to get my utility knife. I picked it up, walked back to him, and slashed him across the chest. He screamed loudly and then sucked in air through his mouth. I said, "Yeah, you like that huh, you like that?" I cut him again, but this time across his face. The razor opened his face up like hot plastic being melted. Shawn screamed as the blood ran constantly out of his jaw. I asked in a calm and soothing voice, "Where the dope at Shawn?" He took too long to answer so I hit him again with the blade, but this time across his other chest muscle and rotator cup.

He screamed again and I waited until he finished and then I asked, "Are you ready to talk about Eric and the warehouse?" He begged me to let him go. He said I had all of the money and the coke and asked that I just let him go. I nodded and hit him again with the razor across his stomach. I said, "It's up to you my nigga how far we take this."

As he finished grunting and shaking, I told him that I would let him bleed out in that motherfucker if he didn't tell me what I wanted to hear. He closed his eyes and fought through the pain so I hit him across the back with the box cutter a few times. He jerked and wiggled, but it was no use. I walked over to my Kroger bag and got out the box of salt. I poured salt all over his cuts and wounds and watched him go crazy. I asked him if he was ready to talk and he said he didn't know nothing. I warned him, "What I tell you about that bro shit?" I told Tre to get the extension cords out of the bag and pass them to me. Tre'Von took the cords out and handed them to me. I walked behind Shawn and started whipping him with them. He screamed in excruciating pain as the extension cords tore the flesh from his already bloody back.

Four powerful hits from the extension cord, and he yelled, "Okay, okay, I'll tell you what I know!" I smiled and said, "Now we're talking!" I walked to the front of him and wiped some of the blood from his eyes. "What you got to say," I asked? Shawn gave up the information he said Eric's warehouse was on Dickerson Road by the McDonald's and the intersection. I called him a bitch ass nigga and told him that I didn't believe him. I hollered for Tre to bring me the lighter fluid and BBQ fire starter out of the bag. Tre'Von dug through the bag and quickly found what I needed. I removed the little red cap and squirted lighter fluid all over Shawn's dick and balls. He started begging, "Please, no please don't! I'll talk!"

I told him this was his last chance and then it was going to be it. I asked him again where Eric lived. I asked for Eric's address and where the warehouse was. He responded that Eric lived in Brentwood and the warehouse was in fact located on Dickerson Road by the intersection and McDonald's. I got pissed off and went to the corner of the warehouse. I came back with a broom and broke the handle over a piece of old sewing machine; I rammed the smooth end of the broom handle up his ass and he hollered like a bitch. I asked again, "Where is the warehouse?" He stuttered as he repeated Dickerson Road. I squirted lighted fluid on his dick and balls and down his legs. I made a puddle at his feet and then a trail leading away from him and struck a match. I asked for his last answer and he changed his answer. He said the warehouse was off of Bell Road and Nolensville Road. I asked for the number to the storage and he said eighty-four. I asked for Eric's cellphone number.

I began to lose my patience and started yelling, "What's Eric's number? You deaf pussy ass nigga? What's his fucking number?" Shawn responded, "it's 6-1-5 fuck you!"

"Wrong answer," and I struck another match and asked the question again. He lifted his head up and said, "Death before dishonor!"

I said, "Yeah, I know that sounds good but let's see if You really mean it!" I struck another match and tossed it toward the puddle of lighter fluid and watched it spark up into red and blue flames. A few blinks of the eye and the fire was working its way up Shawn's leg unto his dick and balls. He screamed and hollered as I laughed. As the fire ate through his skin, I started squeezing lighter fluid onto Shawn's body. The fire burned even more and Shawn screamed and begged louder. I was tired of hearing his bitch ass mouth so I walked over and slit his throat with the utility knife just enough to choke him out with his own blood. I took the crowbar that we used to break the window and hit him across the back of his head and blood splattered all over my face and shirt.

I turned to Tre'Von and told him to grab everything we brought into the warehouse and let's go. Tre'Von grabbed the bag and we left out as quickly was we came. Tre'Von told me that we should set the building on fire so we would be absolutely sure that we didn't leave strands of hair, finger prints, or DNA. I was in agreement. So I move to the truck and removed the gas. I filled up two glass bottles with gasoline and stuffed pieces of my bloody shirt into the two bottles. Tre'Von ran to the back of the warehouse to toss them into the broken window. I started putting all of my torture tools back into the trunk of the car. Just as I shut the trunk, I turned toward the warehouse and it was blazing fire.

I stared at the fire with a big grin on my face. As I turned, I felt a gun to the back of my head so I froze. I heard a voice instruct me to put my hands up, lock them on the back of my head and turn around slowly. I did as I was told as I thought to myself, "Who is this asshole?" As I turned to face him, I heard the sound of his radio and I knew he was a Joelton police officer.

I asked, "What's the problem officer?"

He responded, "Just put your god damn hands on your fucking head and don't move you fucking nigger."

I said, "Take it easy man, what's yo problem?" The officer told me I was under arrest for trespassing and arson. He put the handcuffs on one of my wrist and then I heard a shot ring out as a bullet whistled past my face. The officer hit the ground and that allowed me to draw my gun but when I turned around, he was already dead. Tre'von yelled from the darkness behind the warehouse. He asked me if I was alright. I said yes and I asked him where he learned to shoot like that. He reminded me that he was going to be a police officer one day. I told him to help me find the key to the hand cuffs. He found the key and removed the cuffs from my one wrist. As we hopped into the car, I was hoping the officer didn't call for back-up so I started to speed. Ten minutes later, we jumped onto the highway and head back toward Nashville. I was glad Tre'Von's aim was perfect because an inch or two more and it would have been my head busting wide open instead of the cop's head.

I looked over at Tre and he just stared out of the window the entire ride back to the Bricks. I looked at my watch and realized it was almost time for sunrise. I got off on the 28th Avenue exit by Hadley Park and drove over to Charlotte Pike. I went down Charlotte until I was over Park Avenue. I took the car back to Skyview, unloaded the torture tools and knocked on the crackhead Shirley's door. She answered the door on the third knock. I handed her the keys and another hit of crack and she was very happy.

I jumped into Tre'Von's Suburban and we headed over to 39th Avenue to see how much money and dope we had hit for from Shawn's house. Once we arrived at the house on 39th, I got the coke and the money out of the stash. I thought the coke was only three keys because I had a total of three bricks. As I started unwrapping the tape and saran wrap, I realized the bricks were double stacked. What looked like three keys of coke, turned out to be six.

Tre'Von was counting the money so I started helping him count because I was anxious to see how much was there. Tre'Von counted out seventy thousand dollars. I had another fifteen thousand on my side. I quickly added the total up and smiled. I told Tre that we would be splitting the money and six keys down the middle.

Tre'Von responded, "Naw Jay, I don't want the drugs. Just give me the money and you can have all of the drugs." I asked him if he was sure because the drugs were worth way more than the money. He said yea I'm sure. I can use the money to pay for my college and to buy a better car. I told him fuck college, come ball with me and we could take over the city. We would be larger than the Brick Boy Mafia niggas. Tre'von said he wasn't a drug dealer and that he was going to be a lawyer and at the rate I was going, he said I would need one. He said this life isn't for me and this life doesn't last long.

"Whatever Mr. High and Mighty! I'ma ball til I fall, so see ya," I said! Tre took the money and headed toward the door. I put the coke back into the wall and went to get some sleep.

Chapter 8

THE ENTIRE DRIVE HOME, my mind was a wreck. I couldn't believe that I killed a cop and watched Je'Von torture and murder those people. I was happy to have the money that I needed for college, but I didn't want to earn it that way. Now I have to prove how I earned it which would means I had to launder the money.

As Tre'Von started to beat on his steering wheel with his fist he said out loud, "Fuck! It's never easy when you are trying to do the right thang in life!" I had started to hate myself for even getting involved in that mess with Je'Von. I should have just called the police when I found out who the guy was. I sat in the truck trying to clear my mind of the dead cop and the tortured body of Shawn. After twenty minutes, I started to realize that the sun was about to come up so I pulled myself together and headed into the apartment.

I unlocked the door and entered. I was glad that Cookie was still asleep. I quickly went to shower. I turned the water on and stepped inside. My mind had started to play tricks on me and I was losing sight of reality. All I could see was Shawn's bloody body and I was covered in his blood. I tried hard to scrub my body, but the blood seemed like it wasn't coming off. I turned the water knob to the hottest that it would go and continued scrubbing my body. The blood was still there so I started to panic. I felt a hand on my shoulder and spun around and realized that it was Cookie stepping into the shower with me. She asked me if I was okay. I tried to assure her I was fine. She didn't believe me because she said I didn't look like my normal self and she asked why the water was so hot. She tried to avoid the hot water by stepping behind me. I reached out to turn the water down a few notches and I noticed that my body was bright red from the hot water and intense scrubbing.

Cookie took the wash cloth out of my hand and started washing me from head to toe, but I wasn't there with her because my mind was totally out of it. She was trying to give me some head but my dick just wouldn't get hard. She put it in her mouth and sucked on it two or three minutes but quickly realized I wasn't responding. She stood up and asked, "Baby, what's wrong?" I snapped out of my trance and dryly answered, "I'm exhausted." She asked me if I wanted breakfast and I told her no because I was headed straight to bed. Cookie had a worried look on her face so I gave her a reassuring kiss on the forehead and told her I would feel better once I slept for a few hours.

We dried off from the shower and headed over to the bed. I sat down on the bed and she sat on my lap and kissed all over my neck and chest and I held her close to me. We laid down together for nearly twenty five minutes then she got up and went to the kitchen to fix breakfast. I continued to lay with my eyes closed because my mind was racing a mile a minute. Before I even realized it, I was fast asleep. She came into the room and pulled the covers over my naked body and then headed out of the door to work.

I slept over six hours in a peaceful sleep until my cellphone started ringing. I searched for it on the table, found it, and answered it. It was my cousin Black calling to find out what I was up to for the day. I told him was going to go job hunting. He asked me why cause the white man wasn't going to pay me nothing but minimum wage while they used me like a black slave. I told Black I didn't have time for the foolishness and I asked him when he was going to realize that it's 2013 and not 1940. He said You need to get with the program and my response was what program is that. He said the hustling tip because that was the only way I was going to come up out of the jungle. I told Black he sounded like Jay's black ass and the both of them needed to get their lives together because the shit that they were doing won't last forever and they both needed to get out while they could. Black change the subject by asking, "How is Aunt Pearlie Mae doing?"

"I haven't talked to her in a week or so but I guess I 'ma stop by there today," I answered then I asked him how his mom was doing and he said his mom was still the same, still bitching and complaining as usual. I asked him to tell my favorite aunt that I loved her and that I would get by soon to see her. Black said he'd tell her when he talks to her again. I reminded him not to forget.

Black changed the subject by asking me what's going down at Limelight tonight. I immediately told him to forget about it because I wasn't going to the club. He said Nicki Minaj is going to be there and You know how fat that ass is going to be in person. I asked Black, "Is that all you think about?" He responded by saying, "Don't front! You know you like Nicki Minaj and you know she be killin' shit." I had to admit that Young Money/Cash Money was killing shit right now. If I knew how to rap, I would probably be signed to them as well.

Black said, "Yeah that nigga Birdman is winning right now."

"What time is the show tonight, I asked?

"Around eight o'clock," Black answered. I asked Black if there was going to be an after party because, if so, that's where I want to be especially if Nicki was going to be walking around. Black said he would find and out and get back with me. I told him to do that and thought to myself, "Cookie would kill me if I went and hung out with Nicki Minaj but didn't take her. I hung up with Black and walked to the kitchen where I looked in the microwave to find that Cookie had left me a plate of eggs and cheese, sausage and biscuits. I set the microwave for one minute and a half and then open the fridge. I poured me a tall glass of Tropicana orange juice and waited on the microwave to chime. As soon as I heard the chime, I removed the food and began eating

I was halfway finished when I realized that I hadn't put the strawberry jelly on my sandwich. I got the jelly out of the fridge and squeezed it on the remainder of my sandwich. Once I finished eating, I washed my plate and glass and I headed to the bedroom to get dressed.

I was hoping my mom was on her break and could answer the phone when I called her to see what she was up to. The phone rang three times and she finally answered. I wasted no time talking. She told me her transmission had gone out and the warranty didn't cover the cost. I asked her how much it was going to cost to get it fixed. She said she let the car go back to the car lot because she wasn't going to continue to pay a four hundred dollar car note a month for a car that she couldn't drive. I asked her if she called Je'Von for money for a new car. She said she didn't want none of his dirty drug money to buy nothing. I felt bad for my mom because I knew that she tried so hard to be independent and strong.

I needed the money that I had just gotten from the Shawn situation but I couldn't let my mom do bad considering she was the only positive thing I had besides Cookie. I asked, "Ma, do you need me to help you with a car?"

"No baby, I know you need your money for college. I can't take your money. I'll take the bus to and from work," she responded.

"Come on Ma, the bus? You don't have to catch the bus. How about I give you my truck," I asked?

She responded, "That truck is entirely too big for me to drive and besides the gas prices will kill me on a car like that." I agreed with her because gas was three fifty per gallon and the price was steady rising daily due to the war and the assassination of Osama Bin Laden.

She said, "Yeah, I'm glad President Obama finally got him. Maybe things will get better for the US economy." I agreed, "It will Ma, but it going to take some time." I told Mom that I had some extra money to spare so she wouldn't have to take the bus. She was glad to hear that. She thanked Jesus that she was blessed to have at least one thoughtful and responsible son. I smiled through the phone when I heard her words. I felt a bit bad because if she knew how I got the money, then I knew she wouldn't have accepted it and I also knew that she would have been highly disappointed in me. I told her not to worry and to be expecting me in forty minutes to an hour.

I brushed my teeth and washed my face and then I headed out of the front door. I stopped at the gas station and put a hundred in the gas tank of the 'burban. After I filled up, I hit the interstate where the traffic wasn't bad. It only took me twenty-five minutes to get to West Nashville. I pulled up at my mother's house and quickly walked into the house. She smiled as I came through the front door. I walked over to her for a big hug. She hugged me back and kissed me on the cheek. She asked me if I wanted lunch, but I told her I had just eaten not long ago.

I asked my mom what kind of car she wanted. She said she didn't quite know yet, but she knew she didn't want anything too fancy or too big. I told her maybe a Chevy or a Toyota would work for her and she agreed those were great choices for cars. I told Ma to grab her purse because we were going car shopping.

I helped her into the 'burban and we took off. I thought about going back to Africa Motors then I decided against doing that. We ended up going to Bill heard Chevrolet to check out their pre-owned vehicles. We walked around the lot until my mom spotted a car that interested her. She opened the door and sat inside the car and she instructed me to look under the hood. I opened the hood to take a look at the motor and it seemed to be in great shape.

A salesman walked up to us and asked us if he could help us. My mom asked to test drive the car and he said he would go get the keys. He only needed her driver's license to make a copy. We followed him into the building and went to get the keys. My mom gave him her license when he returned, he made a copy and gave us the keys to car.

As we pulled off of the lot, I told mom to put it on the highway so we could see how it performed. She merged into the highway traffic and she pushed the gas pedal. The car handled very well up to sixty and beyond. I looked over at the mileage and noticed that the miles were pretty good so I told my mom lets go back to the dealership to negotiate a deal.

It took a few minutes to get back to the lot. We parked the car in the same spot and headed in the building to see a salesman. We quickly found the same salesman who gave us the keys and he was surprised to see us back so quickly. He asked us what we thought about the Impala. My mom told him that she liked it and then asked the salesman what was the best price he could give on it. The salesman said the asking price was sixteen-two, but if she qualified on the credit, then he could do something like twelve-eight. I interrupted and told him to get the paperwork ready. He asked if we needed financing and my mom said yes, but I said no, we'll pay cash.

The salesman said that was great and it would only take him a few minutes to start the paperwork. He rushed off to get the paperwork in order and mom turned to me and said, "Tre'Von, why did you tell that man that we were paying cash?" With a concerned look on her face, she continued, "Boy, I don't have that kind of money. I only have about thirty-five hundred saved up in the bank."

I responded, "Good, do you have your checkbook on you?

"Yes, why," she questioned?

"Write a check for twenty-eight hundred and I will pay the rest."

"Are you serious baby because that's a lot of money?"

"Ma, it's okay. I got you plus I don't want you to have a car note."

My mom was so happy, she responded, "oh baby thank you and I promise I will pay you back somehow."

"Ma, don't be silly. You are my mom and I love you. You don't have to pay me back." She questioned me about college but I told her not to worry about it.

Mom wouldn't let it go and she continued, "I know that is your college money and I don't want to be taking your money away from you. I know you have dreams and I want you to pursue them."

"Ma, it's okay and I'll be alright. It makes me feel good to know that I can help you." She squeezed my hand and I smiled then I excused myself to the restroom.

I went to the bathroom and pulled my money out. I counted out one hundred one hundred dollar bills and put them on the other side. I returned back to my mom and handed her the money. She looked at the money in disbelief. The salesman came back with all of the paperwork for my mom to sign. She eagerly signed the papers and he asked for the money. She counted him out the ten thousand in cash and then went into her purse and wrote a check for the remainder. The salesman shook both of our hands while handing over the title and the keys to the car. He also gave my mom the Carfax report and warranty papers and thanked us again.

We left out feeling good. My mom went to her new car and I walked over to my Suburban. As she drove out of the lot, I followed behind her until we got back to her house. On my way to her house, I thought about school and my career as a lawyer. I knew that I would need way more money than forty thousand to make it all the way through school. I knew that I could apply for financial aid and probably get approved, but then I would have to pay it back for the first part of my career and could leave me penniless, so I decided to go with plan B.

Once I arrived back at my mom's house, I sat down to have a talk with her. I told Mom that I was tired of seeing her living out west in government housing. She told me that she was saving for deposit on a house, but since she had to spend the twenty-eight hundred from her bank account, that became a minor set-back. I told her not to worry because I had a plan. She smiled and just said okay and she said she believed in me. I gave her a hug and then I left. I drove over to

Buchannan Street and stopped at T&T Wireless and bought me a new iPhone and got a car wash.

I sat back and enjoyed the view because Lil Jimmy had about ten girls in G-strings and thongs washing cars. I made a mental note to come back whenever I needed a car wash. It took the girls twenty minutes to hand wash the 'burban and clean the inside. As two girls bent over into the truck with the vacuum cleaners, I got a hard-on. I told Lil Jimmy to go ahead and let them shampoo the inside as well. I watched their every move as I became more and more turned on. I then told Lil Jimmy, "Damn homie, I see why you get all the business!"

Lil Jimmy smiled and said, "I do alright sometimes."

I said, 'I can't tell, that chain must have cost you a fortune." He lifted the iced out B.B.M. medallion up from his chest and said, "What, this old thang? It ain't nothing." He smiled and continued talking, "It looks like they finished with your truck." I gave him a twenty and a ten and told him to give the girls a tip. He responded, "good looking out, pimp."

I pulled off feeling really horny. I dialed Cookie to see if she could get free from work. She picked up on the third ring. I was hoping she could leave, so I asked her when she was going to be off of work and she asked why, thinking something was wrong. I told her nothing was wrong, I just missed her. She said that business was moving fast but she could leave before five o'clock. I looked at my watch and it was close to four o'clock. I said okay and told her I would see her later back at the apartment.

I hung up and decided to go and get me some soul food from Swett's. I went in to eat since I had time to kill. I ordered meatloaf, mac and cheese, mashed potatoes with brown gravy, two dinner rolls, and one slice of chess pie. I took my time and enjoyed my meal. My mother's friend Yvette came in and ordered her a plate to go. I paid for her meal and walked her to her car. I hopped into the 'burban and headed to charlotte pike to check out the latest music at New Life Records. As I entered the store, I asked Lee, the owner what was new and he said, "That City Paper and Lil Wayne."

I bought both of them and kept it moving. I hopped onto the interstate ramp at 46th and West Nashville and headed home. The traffic had started to get heavy around Briley Parkway, so I got off and took the back streets until I finally made it home.

I arrived home about thirty minutes before Cookie, so I decide to take a shower. Once I was stepping out of the shower, she was stepping in the front door. I yelled through the apartment, "Baby is that you?"

She replied, "Yes my love, it's me."

"I'm in the bedroom," I yelled and she walked into the bedroom and gave me a kiss. I instantly grabbed her by the waist and stuck my tongue down her throat. Before she could speak, I started unbuttoning her pants and started removing them.

She said, "baby, let me take a shower first. I been working hard all day." I told her I didn't care about that. I just wanted her to bend over and put her hands on the bed. I stuck my tongue deep into her pussy and started licking. A few moments later she was speaking Korean. It didn't take her long to get her dripping wet and I started sucking on her clit. Her knees started shaking and I smiled to myself as I continued to suck harder and harder. A heavy stream of white sticky juice came out of her and I knew that I had done my job.

She begged me to enter her so I wasted no time doing so because I was rock hard. I closed my eyes and thought about the car wash girls as I started to pound her pussy. Her insides were fitting me like a glove and I was beginning to cum deep inside of her. I shot my load and kept stroking until I was completely soft. I pulled out and she put my dick into her mouth and sucked it back hard. I laid her on her side and lifted her leg straight up entered her from the back. Each time I stroked all the way into her, I hit her pelvic bone. She asked me to take it easy so I told her to get on top of me.

She got on top and started winding her hips. As she did her thang, I started rocking my hips to her rhythm with each stroke. She closed her eyes and tilted her head back as she continued to grind her clit into my pelvis. She increased her speed and I increased mine. Her breathing got louder and she started speaking Korean once again. My stomach started to tighten up and I closed my eyes and steadied my breathing. She sped up her rhythm again and I started moving twice as fast as she was moving. I started throwing the dick as hard and as fast as I could while keeping rhythm with her. I let out a load moan and she screamed almost in unison. As I started shooting my load deep inside of her, she told me she was cumming. I watched her entire face turn red as she came. Once she was finished, she rolled off of me and laid beside me gasping for air. I laid on my back, waiting for my heart to slow down.

Five minutes later, we started cuddling and kissing. She told me that she loved me and I told the same. I also told her that I needed a favor from her mom if possible. She sat up in the bed and looked at me with great seriousness and asked what did I need. I swallowed hard and I told her that I had fifteen thousand dollars that I saved from when I was working at the strip club. I asked if she thought her mother would loan me fifteen thousand dollars on paper and I would give her fifteen in cash.

Cookie asked, "Why do you want to do this?"

"I want to help my mom get a house and it would help me give her the deposit money that she needs to get the house."

Cookie inquired, "Why not just give her the cash?"

"Because I need to have proof of where the cash came from," She said oh I understand then said okay I will ask her. Before I could speak she said I'm sure she'll do it.

Chapter 9

I WOKE UP FROM my sleep and headed straight to the kitchen to boil a pot of water. I got all of my equipment out of the cabinets and unwrapped one of the keys. I put two hundred and fifty grams in the jar, then added a hundred grams of baking soda. As the hot water hit it, I watch as it fizzled and bubbled. I swirled the jar around a few times and added cold water. Instantly, the coke started to harden and BAM, I had a huge cookie of crack. I swirled it a few more times and then poured the remaining water off. I pulled out my scale and placed the cookie on it to get the exact weight. The scale said two hundred and eighty grams. I sat the cookie to the side so it could dry.

I put another two hundred and fifty grams into the jar and repeated the same process, but this time, I added seventy-five grams of soda. The coke whipped up faster than the first batch and when I weighed it, it was two hundred and sixty-five grams. I put the remaining half of key into the jar and added seventy-five more grams of baking soda. The end result turned out to be a total of six hundred and twenty grams. I let the product air-dry and then I weighed all of it at once and I smiled when the scale read one thousand one hundred and seventy-three grams. I was only seventy-seven grams short of an extra quarter key. I re-filled the pot with more water and let it boil and then I busted open another key and started cooking again.

It only took me twenty minutes total to finish cooking the second key and I got back one thousand two hundred fifty grams. I busted a third one and repeated the process until I was finished. I got one thousand two hundred and sixty-five grams off of that one. I got a pen and paper to do the math. My grand total was three thousand six hundred an eighty-eight grams of crack. I was three hundred and twelve grams away from another free key.

I turned the boiling water off and poured the water down the sink. I put the pot in the sink and sat down at the kitchen table. I started bagging the crack up into twenty-eight gram bags. I had one hundred and thirty-two ounce bags and one half ounce, plus six grams. I cleaned the scale off and headed back to my bedroom.

I got dressed and headed to the bathroom to wash my face and brush my teeth. I called up my dawg Black Obama and my cousin Black. As soon as I got them on the phone, I told them that I had the work cheaper than anybody so they should get at me. Black Obama said cheaper than ten-fifty an ounce and I told him that I had 'em for nine-fifty an ounce, hard or soft. My cousin Black told me that he would slide through and I told him to get at me.

I got my paper from the table and wrote down the calculation to see just how much money I stood to make. 950 x36 = $34,200 @ 3 keys =102,600 plus the 950 x 24 ounces = $22,800 plus 20 grams @$50 =$1000. My total profit should equal $126,400. I stared at the figure on the paper and smiled because I knew that I still had another three keys to cook up so once it was all over and done, I knew I would have at least a free two hundred and sixty thousand dollars from the caper. I was so glad that Tre'Von chose the cash over splitting the money made from the coke. Finally the street was about to be mine. I thought to myself, "as soon as I finish all of this, I'm going to find that Eric nigga and hit his warehouse for the rest of his coke and his money."

I stepped outside on the block to see what was going on in the hood. I let a few niggas know that I had the work for the low and I kept it moving. I decided to go over to Rabbit's house to see what was popping at his spot. As soon as I walked through the door, Rabbit's junky ass asked me for a hit. I told him, "What the fuck this look like nigga, a motherfucking free crack line?"

He said, "Aw Jay Rock, don't act like that. It's a lot of money coming through here and if your shit smoke good, then you can take care of my people." Since he put it that way, I opened the bag with the six grams in it and broke him off a small sample hit.

He put the rock on his glass pipe and lit it up. I watched the pipe fill up with a white cloud and he pulled as hard as he could on the pipe and the smoke quickly entered into his lungs. When he was finished, his eye got big as golf balls and he started choking as he exhaled. He shook his head, giving me the "yes" motion as he continued to choke. Once he was able to speak, he said, 'That's some of the best shit around here! Where you get that from?"

I lied "Miami nigga why the fuck You asking so many questions"?

Rabbit's mouth started rocking from side to side and he stared off into space for a moment. He told me to have a seat and don't go nowhere. He ran upstairs and came back with a twenty dollar bill. I gave him two dime rocks and he broke off one then quickly ran back upstairs. A few moments later, a white bitch came down and bought a twenty and it started from there. I sat at Rabbit's house for an hour or so and before I even realized it I had sold the whole six grams. I counted my money and it totaled six hundred and forty dollars.

I went back to get two more ounces and posted back up at Rabbit's house. He wanted me to serve him for six dollars in loose change. I told him to keep that shit and stop bothering me. I watched his crooked jaw keep moving from side to side and burst out laughing. He wanted to know what was so funny and I told him he was an ugly ass nigga. I gave him a hit for six dollars in change and I laughed at him as he rushed off to smoke it.

A few crackheads knocked on the door and Rabbit's ole lady let them in the house. A toothless white woman wanted a hundred dollar worth and the two black dudes that were with her wanted twenty a piece. I gave the white girl ten dime ricks and two dime rocks to each guy. They all headed upstairs to smoke their shit as I stuffed my money deep into my pockets. Rabbit came back and wanted another ten dollar piece so I broke him off and collected my money.

My phone vibrated in my pocket so I removed it and answered it. It was Black Obama calling to tell me that he wanted to buy three ounces for twenty-eight-fifty. I told him to meet me over at dope fiend Rabbit's house. He said that he was on his way. I ran over to the spot and grabbed what he wanted and five minutes later, he knocked on the door and I let him in the door. He asked me if I had a scale and I said, "Yeah why, you don't trust me?" He answered, "Hell naw nigga, you be pulling stunts and shit!"

I said, "Damn dawg, you know we betta than that." He said, "Yeah, I know but I still want to see it on the scale." So I pulled out my black digital scale and gently turned on the power button. Once the scale balanced out on zero, I placed a dollar bill on it to see if it weighed a gram. It weighed one gram so we both knew that it was accurate. I placed the ounce on the scale in the bag and it read twenty-nine grams. Black Obama quickly asked me was that a double sandwich bag or a single and I told him to stop tripping, it was a single. He said he was just checking because he needed all of his product. We both knew that double pleaded bags weigh more so I laughed and said it's all good my nigga.

He watched as the other two ounces were weighed up and then he gave me my money. He said" how the shit smoked"? I told him to ask any of the crackheads that were in here. They will tell You about it. He called Rabbit into the room and asked him about the quality of the dope. Rabbit put his stamp of approval on it and then asked for a hit since we made the transaction in his house.

I continued to count the money that Black O had just gave me while he argued with Rabbit. As Black O was about to leave, I called out to him and he stopped and turned around. I said, "Man you fifty short! Let me get that!"

He smiled and said, "I was just trying to see if you were up on your shit!"

"Damn nigga! I'm already saving you over a hundred on each ounce and you still tryna short me," So I said shid You the slick one I got to watch Yo ass.

Black O said, "If I don't get you before you get me, then it just wouldn't feel right."

"Yeah okay, I 'ma remember that the next time you need me to look out for you." He told me he was out and I told him to hit me up when he needed some more of that fire. He headed out of the front door and I sat back on the couch. The dirty looking white girl with the missing teeth came from upstairs and asked for another hundred dollar worth. I gave her another ten dime rocks and she was happy. I stuffed the money into my pockets and thought, "the money is flowing like water."

I knocked two roaches off of my pants leg and kicked my feet up on the coffee table. Rabbit's ole lady came in to the room and asked for some Lortab pills. I told her I didn't have any. She asked for a seven dollar hit of crack. I told her You need more than seven dollars if You asking about some pills. She said the pills were for one of the dudes upstairs.

I asked her to go to the store me. She asked me what I wanted and I told her to get me one bag of Cool Ranch Doritos, a bag of Nacho Cheese Doritos, a jungle juice, and a box of Little Debbie Oatmeal Cream Pies. She asked for the money and I told her to buy it with the seven dollars that she wanted to spend and she headed out of the door.

My stomach started growling and I couldn't wait for her to return. A few more smokers knocked on the door and Rabbit let them in to cop. I served them a twenty and fifteen dollar piece and then they left. Rabbit's girl returned with the snacks so I gave her a nice lil hit for the seven dollars she had spent at the store and I mixed the Doritos together and started eating. I smashed four Little Debbie cakes back to back and then popped open the jungle juice. My phone rang so I answered it. My cousin

Black said he wanted to get a key so I told him to meet me at the house. I gathered all of my snacks up and I left. As I was stepping out of the front door, Rabbit ran out and asking where are You going. I told him that I'd be back later because I had something to handle. His mouth was still twitching from side to side as he hollered out the door, "It's plenty of money in the house, don't leave just yet!" I hollered back, "Chill for twenty minutes and I'll be back!" rabbit looked at me like twenty minutes was the end of the world so I let him know that I was going to go cop some more work and I would be right back as soon as I get it in my hands. He softened up a little and said okay and they'd be waiting on You. I told his junky ass that I had his back as long as he kept them spenders upstairs smoking until I got back.

I turned and walked off. It only took me three minutes to get to the house. I pulled out a bird for Black and sat on my bed. I pulled out all of my money and started counting it to see what I had made so far. I put a thick rubber band around the money and stashed it in the heating vents. I ate two more Little Debbie cake and then Black knocked on the front door. I opened the door and he stepped in and gave me some dap. I asked, "What up cuz?"

"Not shit cuz but the paper I'm holding," he replied. I rubbed my hands together and said, "Yeah, I like the sound of that."

"Where Aunt Pearlie Mae," he asked?

"She at work," I responded.

"Damn dawg, she always at work! When do she ever not work?" I told him, "Somebody go to pay the bills around this motherfucker and she know that so that's why she always at work!" I then said, "Let's go to the kitchen." He followed me to the kitchen and we sat down at the table. I pulled the brick out and sat it on the table and said, "Here you go dawg . . . one hundred percent fish scale!"

Black pulled out a black Crown Royal bag and dumped a bunch of hundreds on the table. I went straight to counting and he asked for a sharp knife. I told him to look in the drawer by the sink. He went to the drawer, opened it, and pulled out the knife with the sharpest tip on it and returned to the table. He cut a triangle into the duct tape wrapping of the key. I kept counting the money as he inspected the quality of the coke. I watched him dig a small piece out and crumble it on the back of his hand and took a snort. He repeated the same process with his other nostril and asked where You get this shit from. I told him Peru and then I asked him why he was asking. He said because his nose was already draining. I told him that's what it's supposed to do when it's good shit.

After I finished counting the money, I told Black that it's plenty more of it if he needed it. HE said he would be back for more A.S.A.P. Before he got up to leave, I asked him if he had some smoke and of course he did. I asked him was it any good and he said it was the best. I asked him what he wanted for an ounce and he told me because I was cuz, he'd let me get one for four hundred. I gave him four hundred of his money back and went to get my scale. He had at least a quarter pound of Purple haze on him. He weighed up twenty-eight grams and told me to enjoy.

I went to get a cigar and I quickly split it open and dumped the tobacco into the trash. I broke the ounce down into four quarter ounces and bagged up three. The last quarter I stuffed it in the blunt and rolled it up as tight as I could get it. As I walked Black to the door, CJ and J-Bo were walking up to the porch. I gave them dap and asked them what was cracking. They said Black Obama told them about the work and they wanted in. I asked what they wanted. CJ wanted to get a big eight and J-Bo wanted to buy a half of a key, hard. I told them the price was in ounces no matter what they wanted.

CJ responded, "Damn nigga, we your boys!" and J-Bo co-signed, 'Yeah my nigga, give me the half for fifteen." I let them niggas know, "No-can-do my brother! I got the cheapest work out here besides them Brick Boy Mafia niggas."

CJ quickly changed his tune and said, "A'ight dawg, let's do it." J-Bo kept complaining about the price until I finally said then don't fucking buy it then. I served CJ and I told J-Bo to holl'a at me if he changed his mind. He knew I was serious so he caved in and tried to negotiate. He said, "Check this out, I got fifteen thousand right here and let me owe you the rest." I agree to do that for J-Bo cause I knew he was trying to come up. He got hyped and he said as soon as he get right, he was going to come back through with the grand, but I told him that would be more like twenty-seven hundred and he was like, whatever, he got me. I gave him the half of brick of crack and quickly counted their money. It was all there so I told them to get at me and we all went our separate ways.

I headed back to Rabbit's house to see what I had missed. As soon as I got over there, he asked me why it took me so long to come back. I had to tell Rab chill and stop acting like I had been gone forever when I had only been gone for thirty minutes. HE said it seemed like longer I asked him what he needed. He asked for a fifty and his girl wanted another thirty. The toothless white girl asked me if I wanted to turn a trick and I asked the bitch if she was crazy. She looked confused at first, but soon got the message when I told her to get the fuck out of my face. The two black dudes came downstairs to spend twenty a piece.

Soon as they went back upstairs, I pulled out my blunt and fired it up. Once the smoke entered my lungs, I started to mellow out and feel good. I smoked the blunt halfway down and then put it out because I was feeling too high. I heard three slow taps on the door and I was too high to move or to answer the door. I moved in slow motion toward the door to answer it. I hollered out, "Who is it?" and the voice on the other side said, "Lisa!" I unlocked the door and let her inside. She wanted to buy a twenty dollar rock, so I took care of her. She gave me a hug and said, "Jay, don't go nowhere, I'll be back soon with your money." I watched her go out and get back in her car as I stood outside on the porch for a moment. I saw my homeboy, Lil E, run up to a car and serve some dope through the window. I told myself, damn this young nigga wild ass shit. As soon as I said that, a police jumped out of an unmarked car and started chasing him down the block. I laughed my ass off and shook my head because the two police officers weren't fast enough to catch him. I dipped back off into the house and chilled until they left.

Since I knew Vice was rolling, I decided to go get chewed up by Jasmine. I searched through my call log and once her name and number came up on the screen, I pressed the button. She answered on the second ring and started cussing as soon as she answered the phone. I listened to her talk shit for five whole minutes and then I told her, "Baby, I'm on my way."

It only took me five minutes to get to her house so she was waiting on me. As I was walking up to the door, she opened it and said hurry up and get in here because the police are everywhere out back. I strolled into the house and asked what happened. She said Lil' Josh dumb ass just served vice some dope and they got his stupid ass.

I sat down on the couch and pulled out the rest of my blunt and fired it up. I asked her if she wanted to hit it, when I finished hitting it and she snatched it out of my hand and asked me what You think? I asked her where her bad ass lil boy was and she said he was with his "no good ass daddy" for the day. I told her that was good because I wanted some pussy. She responded, "You only come over here when you want to fuck! Why don't you just move in with me?" I told her, "Man, don't start that bullshit. Just pass that blunt and take that shit off and make sure that door is locked because if that nigga walk in on us, Im'a shoot the shit out of his ass!"

She said, "He ain't coming over her today, so chill!"

"Lock the door and let's go upstairs!" We headed upstairs to her bedroom. I told her to kill the rest of the blunt and she happily sucked it all up until she could barely hold it.

She went and used the bathroom and then came back into the bedroom. She undressed and I watched as she did so. I came out of my clothes and laid back. She crawled straight between my legs and started sucking my dick with a slow and steady pace. I closed my eyes and laid back like a king. She licked down to my balls and started sucking them. She carefully sucked both of them a few minutes and then she went back to sucking my dick.

The Purp had me hard as a rock and super horny. Ten minutes later, I was ready to beat something. I flipped her over and started sucking on her. She was already wet so it didn't take me to no time to get here where I wanted her to be. I climbed on top and started pumping. She whispered, "Give it to me baby." And I continued to my thing. Twenty minutes later, I was finally feeling like I was about to cum. I stopped and told her to turn over on her side. She started making noises each time I stroked her deeply. It didn't take long for her to tell me that she was cumming and I continued to stroke as she released her load all over my dick. She was too wet because every time I tried to beat it up, my dick would slide out of her. I told her to get in the doggy-style position.

I hammered deep into her with every stroke and she moaned and started to talk dirty to me at the same time. She was throwing it back at me as I threw it into her. She matched my strokes with her strokes and I lost all control and came deep inside of her. The Purp had me feeling like I was Superman. I kept stroking as she continued to throw it to me. Her pussy got wetter and wetter by the minute. I grabbed her by the hair and started fucking as fast I could. She complained about her neck hurting but I paid no attention. I started stroking to the side and she couldn't handle me. She fell flat on to her stomach and I came crashing down on top of her.

I started digging deep into her like Ray J did Kim Kardashian on their sex tape. She started trying to crawl but I pinned her down and pulled her neck back towards me like a wrestling move. She continued to whine and cry but I kept drilling deep into her until I came again. I was covered in sweat and completely drained. As soon as I released her from my grip, she grabbed her neck told me that I fucked to rough.

My mouth was dry and I was out of breath, so I didn't want to speak. I laid there and caught my breath and she tried to get her neck right. My cellphone rang and she almost broke her neck trying to answer it before I answered it. I beat her to the phone and quickly looked at the screen. It was my dawg, T-Mac calling me. He asked if I was going to the Nicki Minaj show and I told him Hell yeah I would be there. We chopped it up for five minutes and then I hung up.

I put my clothes on and rushed down the steps. Jas ran behind me fussing and cussing and I ignored her. I got to the bottom of the steps and looked up at her and a shoe came flying toward my head. I ducked and told that bitch she was gonna get her ass beat.

I walked up by the corner store and caught a few crack sells and then I went into the store to get something to snack on. As I came out of the store, I served two young niggas a gram each and kept it moving. I looked back at them and thought that was a crazy sell because they couldn't be no older then twelve or thirteen at the most. A black Chevy with dark tint came creeping through. I got as low as I could and pulled my .40 Glock out. The window came down quickly and gun fire popped out of the window. From the sound of the automatic fire, it was an AK. I took off running full crank and returned fire at the car. I ran as hard as I could as I watched the AK bullets tear through bricks and cars. I hit the corner and didn't look back.

Chapter 10

SINCE COOKIE WAS MY lady, I decided to break the news to her first to see how she would take it. I told her, "Listen baby, I have been thinking about my future and also my career." She said, "That's good, so what are you going to do?"

I explained, "It will take too long for me to become a lawyer and actually be able to help the needy and make a difference."

She asked, "Well what are you going to do, if not become a lawyer?"

"Right now the job market is terrible and I need to do something quick so I don't want to be just another black man without a job, so I decided that I'm going to go and enroll in the Metro Police Academy to become a police officer." She hugged me and said that it was a great idea. She encouraged me by saying You would make a great policeman. I smiled and asked her if she really thought so and she said yes I'm so proud of You. I smiled and gave her a big hug.

"Let's celebrate by going out to dinner," I said. She went to the bedroom and got her purse and left out of the door. Cookie wanted Chinese or Korean so I said that was cool with me, just tell me where to go. She gave me directions and we headed over to West End to the spot she wanted to go eat. She ordered Chicken Lo Mein and egg rolls and I ordered chicken fried rice, two egg rolls and some chicken nuggets. I asked for sweet and hot Asian sauce and we sat down to eat. She ate with a set of chop sticks and I asked for a spoon.

She laughed at me and I reached out for her hand and started rubbing it. I stared into her beautiful slanted eyes and thought, "God, I'm so blessed to have a sweet and beautiful woman of her caliber. I stole a few more looks at her and then leaned across the table and stole two kisses.

She fed me some of her lo Mein with her chopsticks and I shared a couple of my chicken nuggets with her. We both took our time and ate them as we sat at the table and talked afterwards.

It was only eight o'clock p.m. so I decided to do something special so I told her lets go downtown and hang out. She said okay and we asked for the check. Upon arriving downtown, I found a place to park and we took off on foot. We walked around, hand in hand and enjoyed the bright city lights and the people. After we walked for many blocks, I told Cookie let's go for a horse and carriage ride while pointing toward the carriage. I paid the driver and helped Cookie to get in the carriage. Once we were comfortable into the seats of the carriage, she smiled at me and I stared into her beautiful brown eyes. We kissed a few more times and then she slid closer under my arm and laid her soft body against mine. As the carriage moved slowly through the city, I relaxed and breathed in the night air. I said a silent prayer to God to never let the night end. I knew at that moment that I was going to make her my wife.

We rode around for another hour or so and then the night air started to get chilly so we headed back to our car. I asked Cookie if she wanted to drive but she insisted on me driving. I got behind the wheel and started the car and we exited the parking lot. As we cruised through the city streets, Cookie started unzipping my pants. I looked at her and she smiled. She reached down into my pants and started stroking me. I instantly became hard and she started sucking my dick with a long slow motion. I gripped the steering wheel and concentrated on the road. The slurping noise from her mouth was music to my ears and the grip that her tight little mouth was delivering was bringing me closer and closer to the edge of me seat. I squeezed my muscles tightly together and let out a deep breath as I tried to handle the head that was giving. Two red lights later, I lost the battle. I came deep into her mouth and throat and I felt my entire body shake and tremble. I pulled over and put on my hazard lights to regain control of myself.

She asked me if I wanted her to take the wheel and I said, Yeah and she crawled over and we switched position in the seats and then we headed home. The entire drive home, I was floating on cloud nine and my hormones were through the roof. As soon as we entered the front door, I was on her like bees on honey. She told me that she was spotting and I was crushed. I wanted to finish what we started but I knew that I would just have to wait until she went off. I quickly told her that I understood. She told me that she was just as horny as I was.

I said, "Yeah, but it looked like we will only be cuddling tonight."

She said, "I'm too horny for that so I got an idea." I interrupted her by saying, "I'm not doing it if you are bleeding." She said, "No silly, I'm not talking about that. I have something that we both will enjoy." I sat up and asked, "What is it?" She told me to come on and I would see. She grabbed my hand and escorted me to the bedroom and we got undressed and started foreplay. We started kissing and rubbing. She sucked on my neck and my chest and I kissed on her neck and breast. She kissed down my stomach and then down to my dick and balls. Once I became rock hard, she told me to get the KY lubricant out of the dresser drawer.

I was smiling the entire time as I was searching for it. I grabbed the bottle and I returned to the bed. She bent over in the doggy style position and I started lubricating her up. I took my time and worked my way into her and then I tried to be gentle as possible. Once she had gotten comfortable I increased my pace until I was able to go with a better rhythm. She started speaking in Korean and I got super turned on so I increased my stroke deeper. Her breathing became louder and louder with each and every stroke. She started rubbing her clit as I continued stroking.

She started moaning and I closed my eyes and continued stroking as I started to feel that wonderful sensation rise from my balls. It started working its way up to the shaft of my dick and I increased my speed until I was deep within her. She let out a few screams and I slowed up my stroke. She announced that she was cumming so I loosened my muscle and shot off deep within her ass. As I finished releasing my nut, she laid down on her stomach and I rolled over to my back. Once my heart rate slowed down I stood up to go shower.

She followed behind me and I started the shower water while she removed her tampon. I decided to let her go first so I waited on her to come out.

While she bathed I decided to call my mom and give her the news. She answered on the second ring and I was glad to hear her voice. We talked about ten minutes then I broke the news to her of me going to Police Academy.

I could tell by her voice that she was so happy for me. Her other line started clicking and she said baby hold on. I told her to go ahead and take the call and we would talk later.

We both said goodbye then I hung up as she clicked over to her other line. Cookie was coming out of the bathroom so I went in and showered about twenty minutes or so.

I returned from the shower feeling good and refreshed. I brushed my teeth and got into the bed with her and started cuddling. She backed all the way up to me and I gently kissed the back of her neck then said baby I love you.

She said I love you also. I paused for a brief moment or two then said I got something else I need to ask you. She said what is it baby? I swallowed a few times then said will you marry me?

She rolled over and faced me and said what? I looked into her beautiful eyes and said Cookie will you marry me? She started crying but shook her head yes.

I quickly thought about a ring then said baby I don't have a ring yet but I'll get one tomorrow. She said okay baby I'm so happy. She leaned in and kissed me. I kissed her back and we lay in each other's arms the whole entire night.

I awoke to a breakfast for a king. Cookie had prepared eggs and cheese, toast, sausage, hash browns, and orange juice for me and tea for her. I washed my face and brushed my teeth then I headed to the kitchen.

We sat and ate together and she couldn't stop smiling when I told her that the food was delicious. I know that she had been trying hard to cook like an American so I wanted her to feel appreciated.

I looked at the clock and realized that she was close to leaving for work so I offered to do the dishes. She told me that in her culture the woman is supposed to take care of those chores. I smiled and said don't worry about it baby I'ma do it for you today.

She looked kind of disappointed so I kissed her on the forehead and assured her that it would be okay. She asked me was I sure in her sexy Korean accent and I became turned on. I smiled and said yea I got you.

She gave me a kiss then headed towards the bedroom. Two minutes later she returned with her purse and keys. She gave me a kiss and hug then quickly left off to work.

I finished eating then I quickly washed the dishes by hand. Once I finished I got dressed and headed out the front door. I drove out by Rivergate mall and started ring shopping.

The mall didn't really have nothing so I went to a store called Jared, upon arriving in there I knew that I was finally in the right store. I asked to see some nice engagement ring and the white lady behind the counter smile and said please step right over here.

She asked me did I prefer platinum or gold. I told her gold so she showed me everything gold. I carefully checked out the rings and there price. It took me about thirty minutes to select the one I thought was the best but I chose a two carat ring for $8,900.

The lady gifted wrapped the ring for me and I left. Once out of the mall I headed out west to see if my mom was home. When I got there I quickly discovered that she was at work.

I left a message on a piece of paper and slid it under her bedroom door. I decided to drive over to the police academy to see what I would have to do to become an officer.

Since traffic was lite I got there in no time at all. I spoke with an officer and he told me all about becoming a metro police. He gave me some papers to fill out and bring back.

I shook his hand and thanked him then I left. Once I got back out west police was everywhere. As I passed six cars of police and an ambulance I noticed a section yellow taped off and two bodies under a sheet.

I went back to my mom house and chilled. I quickly thought about Je'Von so I called him to make sure it wasn't him lying under one of those white sheets.

I listened to the music on his ringtone as his phone rang. I sung along to Jeezy's verse. Right when my favorite part was near Je'Von answered.

I was relieved that it wasn't him lying under the sheet so I happily said what's up bro? He said not shit I got a hangover from last night.

I said from last night what happened? He said in a low and groggy voice, I went to that Nicki Minaj concert and I hung out afterwards.

I said Nicki Minaj huh and he said yea I had to go and see my baby it wouldn't have been right if I didn't go to support her. I swear Trey I'ma marry that girl.

I said yea right good luck loco, she don't even know who you are. He said that's okay I got enough money to hire her for a private show. After that she will know who I am because the show will be only for me.

I said yea okay Jay you are drunk for real but it sound good so I 'ma let you believe that madness. I quickly changed the direction of the conversation by telling Je'Von that I was about to marry Cookie.

He laughed and said boy that pussy must be good if you talking about marriage. I said why you always think sex got to be the reason for something?

He said cause nigga it sound like you are pussy whipped ole tender dick ass nigga. I had started to get upset so I said whatever you say. Oh yea and I'm enrolling into the police academy next week also.

Je'Von stopped laughing and said what? I said yea that's right I'm enrolling into police academy. It's a twelve week process, one week for my registration papers, physical examine and six weeks of physical training and a few other procedures.

Je'Von got super quite so I could tell that I had struck a nerve so I said you aint got nothing to say Jay? I thought you would be happy for me.

He said happy for you, nigga I hate god damn cops why should I be happy that you want to be a stanky ass pig? I never ever met on good god damn cop who helped me do nothing. All of them are alike, shit protect and serve my ass.

I said Jay you are out here living wrong, why should a police man help you do anything? You selling poison to your own people in your community.

He said if I don't get that money then all they will do is spend it with those Brick Boy mafia niggas, so better me than them. I said Jay just stop selling drugs and I promise you I will get them all out of the neighborhood. I will personally lock all of them up myself even if I have to put drugs on them.

He said you don't have to become a cop to put them niggas away, we can do that without you being a cop. I said how is that so jay? He said all we have to do is go and get the choppers I got stashed and we take them out one by one all through the city.

I said Jay that's the crazy way of thinking; you can't kill the whole city. He said well you can't lock up a whole city and especially them niggas because it's too many of them. Hell the feds is still looking for mafia and they aint found him yet, how you suppose to get all of them by yourself and the feds can't get the head nigga of the group?

I could see that it was a losing battle so I simply told Je'Von please just be happy for me. He said whatever Trey then quickly said I got to go.

Before I could say okay the phone clicked in my ear. I looked at the screen and shook my head. I decided to go and get something to eat since moms hadn't come for her lunch break.

I drove over to Princess Hot Chicken to get me a hot chicken meal. As usual the line was out the door. I decided to drive downtown and get me a chicken plate from 400 Degrees since Princess was too crowded.

As I rode through downtown I past mafia studios and shook my head. I pulled up at 400 degrees and went in. My order was cooked and prepared within twenty minutes, I paid and left.

As I climbed back into the Suburban my cell rung so I quickly answered it. It was Cookie telling me that her mother agreed to write the check for the cash. Cookie made it perfectly clear that the only reason she was doing it was because she told her about the marriage proposal.

I said Cookie thank you and told her to tell her mother the same. She agreed to do so and then asked me how my day was going.

I told her that it was going good so far except for the disagreement I had with my brother. She said baby about what? I said I broke the police academy news to him and he's not thrilled about it.

She said well baby don't you worry he will change his mind, I'm sure he will support your decision sooner or later. I said I doubt it because he see things his way and his way only.

She said well baby I support you and I'm proud of you so that should be enough. I smiled and said thank you baby that's why I love you.

We talked about an hour then my battery started blinking low battery. I quickly put it on the cigarette cord plug and tried to revive the battery before it completely went out. The cigarette lighter sock it wasn't working and my battery went dead.

I sat in the car and ate my chicken while it was still hot then I headed home to get my extra battery. Upon arriving there I grabbed the spare battery and headed back out the door.

I drove to AutoZone and had them to check the lighter socket. They said that it was only a fuse blown. I replaced it and headed back to my mom's house to wait on her to come home so I could give her the wedding news.

Chapter 11

I PACED AROUND THE floor in circles contemplating whether or not I should kill Tre'Von. I didn't like the idea of him becoming a cop and he being my brother didn't make it any exception to my rules.

I rolled up another quarter ounce of purp that I had bought from black. I took a few pulls on the blunt and I popped a roxy then I started to feel much more relaxed.

I put my clothes on and went to the trap house to see what was shaking. Soon as I got there rabbit was throwing money in my face. I sat up a little work area and started serving.

Twenty and fifty sales came back to back. Fast as I stuffed the money in my pocket Rabbit was back handing me more money. Two hours later I was out of everything.

I told Rabbit to keep all the money in the house until I came back. He asked me how long would it take and I said five minutes. I went up to the stash house and got another key from the stash then headed back.

Once I was back in the trap house I went straight to the kitchen and broke the key down. The crackheads was getting impatient so I decided to cook the crack up in the microwave.

Within no time I had cooked up the whole key. I weighed up piece by piece to see what the total was. I smiled when I found out that I had over forty-two ounces.

I quickly cleaned up everything and went back to serving. Rabbit worked the front door and delivered the crack from me to them. I sat back and collected as the money continued to pile up.

After about another hour had past the sells slowed down so I was finally able to count my money. I quickly counted everything from the first trip. Then I started on everything from this trip. I rubber band my money up in five thousand stacks then hurried back over to my mother's house to stash the money until I was finished serving. Once I arrived back at my mother's house I stashed the paper and rushed back to the trap house.

As I was leaving out of the house I grabbed my phone off of the counter and kept it moving. As I was walking up to the porch Black Obama pulled up and asked me what was good.

I said the same ole thang last time and he put the car in park and got out. I waved for him to come into the house so he followed me in.

He asked for a half of brick so I pulled out the scale and started weighing the ounces up. Once I had weighed and bagged up eighteen of them I handed them to him and he gave me the paper.

He dapped me up then left. I continued counting the money as he headed out of the door. Once I finished counting his cheese, I rubber banded it up and went back to my mother's house to drop that off.

I then walked to the corner store and bought two bags of Cheetos, one regular and one flaming hot. A box of little Debbie cakes, one oatmeal cream pie and one nutty bar wafers, a 20 oz. sprite and six packs of banana, fruit punch and apple now and laters.

I paid the store owner and headed back to the trap house to get my paper. Once there I fired up my blunt and got tore up. The crackheads continued to spend all their money and I was happy.

I texted a few messages then went right back to smoking. One hour later I started to get the munchies so I opened the nutty bars and smashed them by the twos. I mixed both bags of Cheetos together and punished them until they were gone. I drank the sprite halfway down then ate four oatmeal cream pies.

Around four p.m. the sales slowed down and I laid back on the couch to relax. I knew that the police shift had just changed so sales would slow up a little then pick up later once it turned dark.

I logged onto Facebook from my phone and typed a few messages on my wall and to some broads. I read a post from J-Bo then realized that he hadn't paid me my money yet.

I made it a mental note to call him and see what's good with that then I kept poking Sashia, Kimberly, and Alexis. Some white girl sent me a friend request and I denied it and continued checking out Kim photo album.

Once I got tired of that I decided to go outside and see what was cracking in the hood. I walked up on 40th avenue and hung out. Mada came through talking shit and a big dice game jumped off.

I went into the store to get something to drink because I had cottonmouth. I decided to go and get some free money from the dice game so I walked over to where they were and pulled out my paper.

As I got closer to the crowd I noticed J-Bo in the dice game so I told him let me holla at you dawg. He said not right now I'm down and you are breaking my concentration.

He rolled four and scooped up a handful of money from all different directions on the board. I watched him roll five, eleven then seven. The next man picked the dice up and asked who wanted to bet against him.

I told J-Bo once again dawg let me holla at you, he snapped out and said" what can't you see I'm busy nigga what the fuck do you want anyway?"

I snapped out and said WHAT THE FUCK DO I WANT? I want my paper you owe me nigga. He said paper what paper? I don't owe you shit nigga. I said my twenty-0ne hundred nigga—that motherfucking paper.

He said man I don't owe you shit broke ass nigga and anyway that garbage ass dope you sold me wasn't shit so get it like Tyson got it, because I aint got nothing for you.

I said oh yea bitch ass nigga we will see about that then I swung and hit him dead in the jaw. He swung back but missed so I caught with another one but this time his chin.

He almost went down; he caught his balance and shook it off then squared off again. Everyone from the dice game moved out the way but stood close enough to see the fight up close.

I swung at him again but missed so he caught me with a quick two piece. I backed up and shook it off then went back at him. As I swung again he stepped to the side and caught me with another quick two piece and busted my lip.

Blood oozed from my lip and into my mouth. After I tasted the blood I became mad. I spit the blood out and squared back up and waited for him to make a move.

He never swung again so I rushed towards him and he caught me with another two piece before I could grab him. I ate the two pieces that he delivered and kept rushing until I had him in a bear hug.

I slammed him to the ground and started kicking him in his ribs and side. He tried to roll out of the way so I started kicking him in the head and face.

Blood flew everywhere and I started talking shit as I kicked towards his mouth. Some of his gold teeth came out and his partner Rome grabbed me from behind. I bowed him in the nose and he bent over and grabbed his nose as blood poured from it.

I gave Rome a hard right hook to the jaw and he went down. I turned my attention back to J-Bo then that's when I seen him reaching in his waist for something.

I took out running as he came up with a chrome pistol and started firing. Bang bang bang bang bang bang bang bang. The rest of the crowd started running in a different direction he let off more shots then that's when I saw a lady go down and holla.

I ran to my momma's house and cleaned my lip up then got my cash out the stash and headed to the house on 39th. Once I got there I put my money up and got out the chopper.

I went to the kitchen cabinet and pulled out the latex gloves. I pulled two from the box and put them on. I put the box back where I had got them from then I went and got a hundred bullets and loaded them into the drum.

The whole entire time I was loading the drum up I was talking to myself. CJ called me and told me I heard what went down with you and J-Bo, damn that's fucked up.

He said I already know that you are going to ride on them niggas but just chill for now because police everywhere. I said who got hit? He said a little boy got shot, a lady and Wendell grand momma.

I said good looking out with the news, keep me posted if you see him or Rome anywhere. He said will do my nigga, one. I said one then hung up.

I finished loading the AK up and waited for the police and ambulance to leave from 40th. I stayed in the house and rolled up another blunt and started smoking. Soon as seven o'clock came and it started to get dark I hit the streets looking for them.

I went to the trap house and took care of Rabbit and his smoking partners. I proceeded to get my money the rest of the night all the way up until six in the morning.

I closed down shop and went home to get some sleep. I slept up until 12:30 then I got up and answered my cell phone. Black Obama told me that Wendell wanted to holla at me.

He put Wendell on the phone and I could hear the pain in his voice as he asked me what happened. I told Wendell that I'm sorry about his grandmother getting shot and he told me that he knew where J-Bo bitch live at.

He gave me the address and street then told me to come and get him so we could ride together and hunt him down. I told him that I would pick him later around eight o'clock.

He said bet that and I hung up. I called my cousin Black up and told him that I needed another ounce of purp. He said that he was out of purp but had plenty of sour diesel.

I agreed to buy an ounce and told him that I was on my way to get it. I drove over to the eastside of town and picked up the smoke from Black. I chilled with my aunt for an hour then I headed back out west.

I got off on 28th and cut through Geneva Circle; from there I rode up Clifton and turned on 39th. I ran into Rock and he wanted to buy a whole key so I told him to meet me down Rabbit house in ten minutes.

I got the last key out of the stash and headed over to Rabbit house to take care of Rock. Upon arriving there we did the exchange and I kept it moving back to the honey comb hide out.

I pulled out all of my money and started counting it. I was anxious to know what I had made in total. I ran through the paper and it came out to be two hundred and some change. I had a sack of crack that I was serving out of so I weighed it up to see just how much I was working with.

The scale read a little bit over a quarter key. I planned to sell all of that in dimes and twenties so I knew it was time to check out that warehouse caper real soon.

I separated the money into two stacks. I put half of it back into the stash then I bagged the other stack up to take with me. I drove to my storage on Charlotte Pike and stashed the bag in the secret compartment of my broken down old school Chevy.

I stopped at Jack in the Box and bought me a combo meal then headed over to the address Wendell gave me on J-Bo. As I turned off of Charlotte Pike I scrolled through my phone and found the text message with the street and address.

I found the street that I was looking for and slowly drove by the house to scope it off. A thick young girl came out to the mail box. I watched her ass jiggle and shake as she headed back to the house.

I drove off and headed to the East side to find my crackhead cousin Melvin. It took me about an hour to find him but I caught up with him in Delway Villa apartments.

Soon as he saw me he ran up to the car and started begging for a hit. I told him to get in the car. He jumped in and I pulled off down the block and gave him the run down.

He agreed to do what I needed when I told him that I would give him an eight ball of crack and twenty dollars. I took him out west to the house on 39th and told him to chill until the sun went down.

I gave him a gram of crack to smoke while he waited then I sat in the living room and played madden until the sun went down. While Melvin started smoking his crack I went on a short run. I drove over to T& T wireless and bought 2 prepaid throw away phones and minutes.

I headed to sky view and rented crackhead Shirley's car then went back to the house. I parked Shirley's car three blocks from my house and walked over to my house.

Melvin was still in the back smoking, I sat down in the living room and played madden. Around nine o'clock it was good and dark so I decided to go and make a move.

I told Melvin to get all his stuff and bring it with him, he grabbed his pipe and other paraphernalia then we went over the plan. I grabbed my gloves, hat, bandana, and Ak-47 and we left.

We drove over to J-Bo girlfriend's house and the whole street was quite. I parked down the street and we walked between the houses until we was standing in the backyard of her house.

I heard a female voice talking to someone but I couldn't tell who or how many people it was. I peeped through a window and saw a little girl running around playing. She couldn't have been no more than four years old.

I continued staring through the window looking for the voice. After ten minutes or so the same girl from earlier came out of the kitchen and ordered the little girl to sit down and stop running through the house.

I told Melvin to climb up on the roof and see if he could get into the second level of the house. He started climbing after I gave him a boost. I watched him check the windows of the bedroom and shake his head.

He climbed back down and said they are all locked. I said okay then we are going through the door. I said plan b, you know what to do. He walked around the front and gently knocked on the door. I cocked the AK and stood back and watched the window. The woman in the kitchen started towards the front door. I got ready just in case she went crazy. She answered the front door and Melvin asked if J-Bo was there?

She said no he isn't here and Melvin said well do you know when he will be home becuase he told me to bring this stuff over here for him. She unlocked the door and peeped out at Melvin.

He held up a box that the cell phone came in and she opened the door wider. As she reached for the box, Melvin stuck the gun in her face and forced his way into the door.

I ran behind him and quickly came in and locked the front door behind me. I heard Melvin tell her bitch you scream you die. She asked in a low voice what do want please don't kill me.

I said where is J-Bo is he upstairs she shook her head no. I said bitch don't lie because I'll kill your little girl and you. She stuttered between words and said I I I swear he isn't here it's just me and my four year old.

I told Melvin to sit her and the little girl down and watch them while I search the house. I crept up the stairs and quickly scanned all of the rooms and bathrooms then came back down.

I told Melvin that I'm going to the car so keep an eye on them. I backed tracked to the car from the back door. Once at the car I got some tape out of the truck and a box cutter.

I went back to the house and gave Melvin the tape and told him to tie both of them up by the wrist and the ankles. She started crying as Melvin pulled out the tape and wrapped it around her hands then her legs.

Melvin said yo cuz are you sure I should tape the little girl? I said yea tape her to because they both might die if I don't get what I want.

Tears continued to roll down her face when she heard those words. I said listen to me carefully where is J-Bo? She shrugged her shoulders. I remove the tape from her mouth and she said I don't know. I said when the last time you seen him?

She said it's been about two days now, he don't come over here every day but he usually come by at least twice a week to see my daughter.

I said so you his baby momma? She said yes I'm his baby momma. I said what is your name? She said Niecy. I said look Niecy, because of J-Bo I'm thinking about killing you just to piss him off.

She said why me I don't have anything to do with nothing. I said okay I need to call him up and get him over here and we will settle this with him and let you and your daughter go.

She said okay I'll do it, please just don't hurt me and my daughter, I said okay if you do what I tell you then I promise to let you and her go free.

I said what's his number? She called out the number 615-320-1068 so I dialed it and let it ring. No one answered so we redialed it and let it ring again.

The voice mail came on so I told her to leave a message. She spoke into the phone as I put it up to her mouth. She said Jeremy can you please come by the house and bring some cough syrup for Jermilla because she caught a cold.

I pressed the button and hung the phone up and waited to see if he would come. I told her you have two hours or you die so you better hope he show up.

I asked her where was the money and dope? She said that J-Bo doesn't trust her with his money and he's not allowed to bring drugs in the house. I said I'ma tear the house up looking for it and if I find anything in here, I'ma kill your daughter and let you watch her die. She said I promise it's nothing her, but I have three hundred dollars in my purse.

I said that isn't enough so you better be telling the truth because I'ma about to start looking through every inch of this house. She said I swear I'm telling the truth.

I said okay maybe this is what you want to see. I told Melvin to get my pistol and I handed him the ak-47. I put the pistol to the baby's head and said where they money and dope? Before she could answer I said her blood is on your hands.

She said please don't kill her I swear its nothing here. I said yea okay I believe you then lowered the pistol and gave it back to Melvin.

I went to the refrigerator and got some grapes out and started eating them, Melvin said he was hungry so I grabbed him some sliced turkey and cheese and made him a sandwich.

Since he didn't have on gloves I reminded him not to touch anything. I put the bread back in the kitchen and closed the refrigerator then returned to the living room.

An hour had passed and he still hadn't showed up or called to see what was wrong. I redialed the number she gave me and let it ring. After the fifth ring he picked up. She asked him could he please come over and bring his daughter some cough syrup and soup.

He said yea I'll be there in thirty minutes then hung up. I told Melvin to get ready so we could surprise him when he decided to show up.

I paced the floor with the chopper waiting on him to show. Every few minutes I looked at the watch thinking where in the fuck this nigga at. An hour and fifteen minutes past and I was extremely pissed off.

Niecy asked me could she use the bathroom and I said no. I'm not going to untie you so you can try something stupid. She said please I have to use the bathroom.

I said if I let you use it I'm going with you and I'm still not going to untie you. She said okay whatever just please let me go.

I said you better have to pee because I'm not wiping your ass. She said yea I only have to pee. I stood her up and carefully walked her upstairs to the bathroom and pull down her pants and panties for her.

I went into the closet and got a clean wash towel out and wiped myself off on the towel. I untied her hands and told her to get into the bath tub.

She laid on the floor and continued to cry. I put the gun to her head and said bitch get into the bath tub. She slowly got up off the floor and sat on the side of the bath tub.

As she sat down blood leaked all over the floor and bath tub. I uncut the tape around her ankles and ordered her to get into the bath tub then put the gun to her head.

She stepped over into the bath tub and continued to cry. I gave her a wash rag and some soap and told her to start washing up. I watched her wash up then I ordered her to sit down in the bath tub. She sat down so I called Melvin to the bottom of the steps and told him to cut the phone line in the house.

A few minutes later he came back and said okay it's done now what? I said leave out the back door and don't touch nothing, I'll meet you back at the car.

He said okay cuz then walked off. I stood over Niecy with the AK and said bitch I should kill you but I'ma let you live to give this message to J-Bo dog ass.

I said you tell him that his days are numbered and he is a dead man walking. I told Niecy to tell him if he wouldn't have fucked my girlfriend and had her steal my money for him then none of this would have happened. I said tell him he better think twice before he decides to fuck my girl.

I left out of the back door and stuck to the darkness of the houses. Two doors down the neighbor's dog started barking and I took out running as their back porch light came on.

I made it back to the car and pulled off. I took Melvin back to the eastside and gave him what I promised plus a bonus. He was more than happy to collect his money and crack. He said if you need me again cuz you know where to find me. I said okay and sped off.

I took Shirley her car back and broke her off another gram for the car. I jumped back into my whip and pulled off. Soon as I got to the AutoZone I stopped and threw away the towel I used to clean myself with.

I headed back to 39th and changed clothes from all black to dark blue. The clothes I took off I put them into a plastic trash bag and dumped them in the dumpster. I set the dumpster on fire and headed over to rabbits house.

I took care of the crack sells there and sat back and rolled a blunt of sour diesel. I got high for an hour straight, and then I decided to go to the club. I hit CJ and Black Obama up to see if they wanted to ride to club Miami. They both said I will meet you there. I said cool then hung up.

I went and got ready then I headed over to the club. The line was long so I sat in the parking lot and smoked a blunt. I sent out a few text messages and listened to Jeezy spit his dope shit.

My favorite part of the song was coming so I started singing along. "Still use a duck ass nigga for target practices, infrared beam on the Mossberg pump. Hit his ass with it twice and make him A-Town stomp. In gats we trust. A lot of niggas play games dawg but not with us. Call me Jack in The Box hop out with clips, cook yo ass faster than a T-Bone at Ruth Chris. You still hating looking stupid; I'm in a SL looking real coupish.

Sitting 24 inch off the ground, that's how you feel? Young nigga selling fruity by the pound, that's how you feel? And I got the best white in town, that's how you feel?

Just as I looked up I spotted what looked like J-Bo car pull into the parking lot. I waited to it past then I got out the car to see where he was parking.

I quickly got my blue bandana and tied it around my face then I got the chopper out of the trunk. I made sure one was in the chamber and I crept between park cars until I was close to his direction.

He got out the car with some nigga I didn't know and they was walking and talking. I stood up from behind the car and called his name. When he heard his name called him and the other dude looked towards my direction then I let the chopper loose and mowed them both down.

I let off about twenty to thirty shot then quickly ran back to my car as the crowd scattered through the parking lot and into the club. I threw the chopper on the backseat and got the fuck away from the scene.

I was so amped up from the Jeezy playing and from the shooting that I didn't even realize I was speeding. I slowed down and did the speed limit until I was getting off of the 46th and West Nashville exit. I went and put the gun up and change cars and clothes.

I called Jasmine to see if her baby daddy was there and she said no why you always ask me that? I said I'll be there in ten minutes so be looking out for me to pull up.

When I got there she was standing in the front door, I parked and jumped out and quickly strolled to her house. I came in and went straight to the couch and started rolling up a fat blunt of sour diesel.

As we started smoking I turned on the TV to the news to see if it was going to mention anything about the shooting. I watched for about five minutes then the story finally broke, it showed the club, number shell casings and two bodies under bloody sheets.

The news reporter started interviewing a woman who said she had seen the shooting. I paid extra attention to her name as it came across the screen just in case I had to track her down and do her.

They asked her the details of what happened and all she was able to say was the shooter was tall, medium built but stocky. They asked her did she get a look at the face of the shooter or the vehicle and she said no because when the gunfire broke out she broke out in the other direction.

They asked her was there anything about the shooting she could remember of provide and she said no. she gave a shot out to some people and then the reporter switch over to the police chief.

The police chief got on TV and called it a brazen act of violence and said if someone has a lead or information about the case then please call 1 800 Crime Stopper.

I watched the rest of the news then turned the TV off and continued to get high with Jasmine. After we finished smoking I popped two 30 miligram Roxy and we took a shower together.

Upon exiting the shower we went straight to the bed and started foreplay. The pills kicked in and everything felt terrific. I kissed, licked, and sucked on her entire body from head to toe and she returned the favor.

She came four times and I had just started to get my first one. I got on top and worked hard to get my second but it seemed like it was just taking too long.

An hour and a half past, I was covered in sweat and I still haven't got my second nut so I said fuck it and rolled off of her. I laid there and she held me close to her.

I pushed her head down towards the dick and she quickly got the message. She put me deep in her mouth and gave me twenty minutes of none stop head.

Her neck started hurting and her jaws got tired but I made her keep going. She jacked me off with her hand and sucked at the same time. I finally got my second nut right at the two hour mark.

I came all down her throat and I enjoyed watching her swallow it all. She went to rinse her mouth out and I laid back and closed my eyes.

She laid her head on my chest and listened to me breathe. I ran my hands through her hair until I dose off and fell asleep.

Chapter 12

I SAT AT MOM's house for a couple hours and she finally came home from work. Soon as she entered the door she hugged me and told me that she love the car.

I gave her a hug and sat back down on the couch. She said how long you been here? I looked at my watch and said about two, two and a half hours.

She asked me was I hungry and I said no ma I'm good. I wanted to get right down to it so I said look ma then held up the gift wrapped ring and said I'ma ask Cookie to marry me.

My mom was all smiles. She instantly gave me a hug and said that's great Trey, I'm so happy for you. She said it's about time because I have been wanting some grand kids.

I smiled and said slow down ma you are moving too fast, no one said anything about kids yet. Maybe in the future but right now I don't know.

She said child please it will give me something to do besides working all the time. I said its plenty time for that I just want to secure my future first. I want to be stable and able to be a real father to my seed.

She said and a good father you will be, Trey you are the most responsible child that I have, we both know that that other one of mine is gone crazy; I just don't understand that boy.

I said yea he has some issues, don't you know he is upset with me for telling him that I'm deciding on going to the academy? I'm sure if we would have been face to face we probably would have got into a fight.

She said now baby don't you worry about your brother he is into God knows what but I'm sure he loves you and support your decision. I said I doubt it ma but it doesn't matter because I'm happy.

She smiled and patted my hand then said I'm happy that you are happy. It feels good to know that you are happy and your life is moving along in the right direction. What more could a mother ask for?

I said I'm sure that's something else that will make you happier but you will have to wait and see. I said it will be the biggest surprise yet. She tried hard to figure out what it was but I wouldn't give in.

We talked and laughed about an hour and it felt good to kick it with my mom. I knew that she was getting older and I wanted to make sure that she knew just how much I love her and appreciate her.

I got a call from Cookie saying she was on her way home so I told moms I would see her later and call me if she needed anything. She said she would and told me to drive careful.

I headed for the door and she holla'd out don't forget to make some grandbabies. I laughed and said okay ma we will work on that. She gave me a kiss and I left.

Once in the truck I smiled to myself and thought about how funny my mom could be. I thanked God for blessing me with a wonderful mom. I pulled off and headed home to what would be my wonderful wife soon.

As I rode in silence I decided to listen to a little bit of music so I popped in Alicia Keys cd. I was grooving to the song like you will never see me again and I was feeling like maybe my mom was right about starting a family of my own.

When the song unthinkable came on I had to sing along. Alicia had me feeling like loving Cookie and wanting to marry her was the best thang in the world.

I pulled up at the crib and went in to the smell of some good food. I went and washed my hands then walked to the kitchen table and took a seat.

She prepared me a plate and I dug right in. I didn't bless my food or nothing. She watched me eat like a pig for two or three minutes then said baby slow down you shouldn't eat that fast. I said babe its good through a mouth full of food.

She smiled and started preparing herself a plate. After we both had finished our meal she said baby I have something for you. I said that's funny because I have something for you also.

She said what is it? I said no baby you first, you know ladies are first in my book. She leaned over and gave me a kiss then she went and got her purse.

She came back and pulled out a fifteen thousand dollar check from her mother and handed it to me. I kissed her and smiled then I went and got the engagement ring and presented it to her.

She quickly tore the wrapping off the box and opened it. Her mouth was wide open as she gasped for air. I said well what do you think? She finally spoke. She said baby its beautiful, I love it.

I took the ring from her hand and got down on one knee. I placed the ring on her finger and said Cookie will you marry me? She started crying and said yes. I opened my arms and she stepped between them and gave me a big hug.

I smiled and asked her was she happy? She said yes I'm very happy. I thanked her for being supportive of me and also being with me through my hospital ordeal.

She kissed my forehead and said that's what I'm here for. She said baby I love you and I promise to make you happy. I said likewise with me and I also promise to make you happy.

She rushed off to tell her mother about the ring and I went online and took care of some registration papers for the police academy.

Once I was finished with that Cookie wanted to talk about what we would wear for the wedding. She said she would get some wedding books from her mother and I sat back and let her talk.

She was talking so fast that I just sat there and smiled because I knew she was excited. I shook my head yes and no when it was a question because she wouldn't let me get not one word in.

We talked about an hour then we decided to watch a movie together. She wanted to watch sleepless in Seattle and I wanted to watch something with some black people in it so we decided on Love Jones.

We watched that while cuddling together and kissing one another between scenes. Shortly into the movie I dosed off and fell asleep.

The next morning I woke up to a note from Cookie saying I owe her another movie night and I would have to prepare my own breakfast.

I washed my face and brushed my teeth then headed straight to the kitchen and prepared myself a big bowl of Fruity Pebble cereal. I ate almost half a box then finally got dressed.

As I was walking out the door I got a call from the police academy instructor, ha asked me was I ready to enroll into his next class. I quickly said yes and he told when to be there.

I walked out the door with a big smile on my face. Soon as I got into the suburban I called my mom's to see if she had to work. She answered on the third ring. I asked did she have to work and she said no so I told her to stay put because I was on my way over to get her.

Traffic was semi heavy since it was around seven am. It took me thirty five minutes to get there and I was happy once I had arrived. I walked into my mom's house without a care in the world.

Soon as I seen her I gave her a big hug and a kiss. She asked me what was I so happy for? I pulled out the fifteen thousand dollar check and handed it to her.

Instantly she said what is it for and Trey where are you getting all this money from? I didn't want to lie so I simply said ma Cookie mom gave it to us as a wedding present.

She said why are you giving it to me? I said because Cookie and I both agree that you should get your dream house and move out of the hood.

Moms face lit up with a bright smile and she said Trey you mean this is for a house? I said yes ma it a down payment on one. Its time you get up out the hood.

She accepted the check and then grabbed me with a bear hug. I hugged her back and told her you are welcome. When she released me from her embrace I notice she was crying tears of joy.

I quickly told her to wipe her tears and grab her purse because I was taking her out to eat and house hunting. She went to her bedroom and I logged onto the computer and pulled up some home for sale in the one hundred price range all the way up to one hundred and fifty thousand price range.

I printed all of the listing out then we headed out the door. We went to a few open houses and looked around until it was close to 12:45 then we stopped at Swetts Soul food to get a bite to eat.

After eating we drove over to Antioch and caught the open house to a house my mom was really excited about. Everything appeared to look good with the house inside and out and the price was right within our range.

My mom talked to the agent in charge of the house and I continued to check out the back yard. As I reached the backyard my cell phone rang and it was a guy from the police academy telling me that all my scores were very impressive.

He asked me did I have a date to come to the academy and I called out the day and time and he said okay great I see you tomorrow.

I thanked him and then I hung up. By the time I caught back up with my mom and the realtor agent I heard my mom say I can afford up to a ten percent down payment.

The realtor lady told her not to worry about putting ten percent down unless her score was below six hundred. My mom agreed to call her within the next twenty four hours.

We all shook hands then we headed back to the burban. As we drove back to the Westside I decided to call Johnathon to see what he was up to.

He picked up on the second ring. We talked about ten minutes then agreed to meet up at Planet Fitness Gym. I kissed my mom good bye and headed over to the gym.

Once I arrived there he was already there, I parked the burban and went inside. He was just getting off of the treadmill. He asked me did I want to hit some sets.

I said let's do it, so we went over to the flat bench and loaded up the weights on the bar. We took three warm up sets then we started at 135 pounds and worked our way up to 285 pounds. After we finished there we went to the incline bench and did four sets a piece then we called it quits.

We hung out in the parking lot for twenty minutes or so then we parted ways. I headed home to take a shower and get out of my sweaty clothes.

Upon arriving home I jumped into the shower and enjoyed the water. Ten minutes into the shower Cookie came in and joined me so we washed each other up.

Once finished I slipped on some shorts and laid back. She put on some panties and bra and headed to the kitchen and started preparing dinner.

I checked my email and Facebook page then headed in the kitchen. I sat at the dinner table and watched her cook our meal. I was getting turned on watching her cook in her thongs.

She asked from over her shoulder without looking, "baby what are you doing"? I smiled and said nothing love just admiring your beauty. She said yea right it probably more like admiring my booty.

I laughed out loud and said well yea that's what I said; I'm admiring your beautiful booty. She said don't start nothing you can't finish. I said oh you lucky tonight. She interrupted and said I'm off of my cycle and I feel naughty.

I said damn babe you make it hard to say no but I can't tonight because I got to go to the academy first thing tomorrow and start training to see if I can make the cut to become an officer.

She said baby just tell me no and I will understand. I said I'm not saying no but I need my energy for the physical examine and endurance test.

I said baby if you want it then you can have it, I will never tell you that you can't have it. She said okay then I want it. I said okay after dinner. She said uh no I want it now. I cursed under my breathe then said okay sexy.

I waited for her to finish cooking then I scooped her up in my arms and carried her to the bedroom. I didn't waste any time getting straight to the matter at hand.

I pulled her thong to the side and slid right in from the back. She went from semi moist to wet in less than sixteen strokes. The wetter she became I started feeling myself getting worked up.

I started letting my mind wonder off to what police academy training would be like. After that my sexual excitement level dropped and I wasn't no more good.

Before I knew it Cookie was cumming and I was happy because I hadn't came yet. She asked me did I cum and I avoided her question by saying tonight was all about you.

We went and showered together then we sat down and ate together. After our meal Cookie and I viewed some wedding arrangements and dresses.

One hour later I barely could keep my eyes open so I told Cookie that I was going to turn it in early. I pulled the covers over me and laid back.

She put the wedding planner book away and crawled in the bed right up under me. I wrapped my arm around her and pulled her closer to me then gave her a kiss.

She kissed me back then said I love you. I told her the same then said goodnight.

Chapter 13

SINCE I WAS ALMOST completely out of crack I decided to get up early and go scope out Eric's warehouse. I drove over to Bell road and Nolensville Road and checked the spot out.

I came up on a gated storage complex so I figured that it had to be the one I was looking for. I pulled up and walked to a security booth and asked the rental cop a few questions.

He told me that all of the units was currently leased out but check with the manager anyway to make sure. I thanked him and went my way.

As I went back to my car I slick looked around for cameras. I got in my car and drove off heading to Brent wood hoping I could somehow get into the gated community of Eric's.

I got out there and had no luck at all. Brentwood police pulled me over and asked me was I lost. I said that I was looking for a house for sale but I couldn't remember which street it was located on.

I don't really think he bought my story but he allowed me to go without any problems. I quickly got the hell away from there and headed back out west.

I banged out the rest of the crack I had left then called my connect and re-uped on a few keys. Lil Wendell called me and asked me did I see the news from last night?

I said naw why? He said man J-Bo and Squirt got killed at club Miami last night. I sounded shock so I said yo you for real my nigga?

He said hell yea baby boy they got smoked. I said damn somebody got his ass before I could get his bitch ass. Wendell said well now you don't have to worry about getting him. I said yea it looks that way. I said damn my nigga I wanted to get his ass to send a message to these cowards that I'm not playing, but some fucking body beat me to the punch.

Wendell said but it's better that somebody cleaned up a mess for you. I said yea you right then I changed lanes. I asked him did he go to the Nicki Minaj concert the other night.

He said naw I miss that shit. I said yes Nicki did the damn thang. I said log onto my Instagram and you will see all the pictures I took.

Just as I was telling Wendell about my Instagram page my homie J-Shon came and wanted to buy two ounces. I took care of him and quickly counted the money. I gave him some dap and told him to hit me up.

I went over to the trap house to show some love there by blessing them with my presence. Soon as I got there Rabbit and his old lady begged for a hit. I gave Rabbit a dime rock and told him to smoke it with her.

I sat up shop and waited for the sales to come through. I sat there for three hours and only made two hundred and some change. Since sales were slow I decided to take a vacation and enjoy myself.

I called Black Obama up and asked him what's going on? He said not shit tired of boring ass Nashville. I said I know this city is some shit aint it?

He said naw it's alright but sometimes it's just boring, it's not Miami, LA, Houston, or New York. Those cities always have something going on but here it's not always like that.

I said I'm heading out to the Memphis Grizzlies game in a few do you want to go with me? Black O said hell yea Memphis is in the playoffs against San Antonio and I believe that they might win.

I said I don't know about that cause San Antonio is super tough but it don't matter I'm just going down to get away from the ville. Black O said I will be over to your crib in twenty minutes.

I said bet that then hung up the phone. I grabbed a change of clothes and my Glock 40 and put it in the car. I drove to the house on 39th and stashed my scale and crack then headed back over my mom house to wait on Black O to come.

I waited almost thirty minutes before I decided to call him back. He answered on the second ring and said chill nigga I'm out front. I came out of the house and watched him pull up behind my car.

He got out and locked his car up then jumped in with me. I asked him are you ready to ride and he said yea. I cut through Tennessee Village apartments and headed over to the interstate.

I got on at 46th and west Nashville exit and jumped into traffic. Black O asked me was it cool to spark up the blunt so I said hell yea fire that shit up.

He lit the blunt and we started puffing. He yelled out turn the music on nigga I know you got something dangerous in here. I gave him the cd case and he looked through it.

A few minutes later he put a cd in the deck and I passed the blunt back to him. When the cd started playing right away I knew just who it was.

I turned the volume up and let Webbie do his thang. I yelled over the music boy what you know about this Savage Life? He said nigga you aint the only one who fuck with this nigga.

When the song how you riding came on I cranked the volume up another three notches and hit the button on the epic center to give it more hard hitting bass.

After we listened to the entire Webbie cd I put in EightBall and MJG and we lit up another blunt and got right. We rode to the music of EightBall and MJG for over an hour.

We sang every song that came on and I told Black I'm MJG you Eight Ball. He said shit that's cool with me. I said okay don't sing no MJG verse then that's all my part.

He sang all of EightBall verses and I sang all of MJG verses. Once we finished listening to that we put that Yo Gotti mixtape in called Cocaine Music and we rocked to that.

We smoked blunt after blunt like it was nothing. We ran through the whole mixtape listening to songs like walking in Memphis, you already know what it is, night life and Hoody.

When the song Hoody came on I jumped right in and started singing riding through the south cause north Memphis stupid hot, they say the feds out, yea we call them bitches super cops. I and e is the label but it's like a game hoe, serve me out your house then I run back in that same door, all black straps out, you know what I came for. Straight face play okay there yo brains go. 187, 211 all over some foolishness, Yo Gotti North Memphis we be on that bull shit.

I'm so fucking hoody my eyes low I know I'm so full of goodies, nigga I'm so fucking hoody. I'm so fucking hoody my eyes low I know cause I'm so full of goodies.

Soon as we arrived in Memphis we drove straight the North Memphis over to Walkins and Brown. We stopped at the restaurant called Melanie's and got us a hood plate.

We got our food and quickly left because all the niggas was looking shady. We headed over to the Peabody and got two rooms. Black Obama started crying about the hotel prices and I just laughed. He asked me what was so funny and I said you nigga, don't you know the Peabody has the most expensive suits? He said damn nigga we could have went to the motel 6 or the holiday inn or something.

I said nigga it aint nothing but money you want to rob one of these Memphis niggas? He said man you tripping, I said naw you tripping we can go over to White Haven or Douglas and get on it.

Before he could say something I bust out laughing and said naw bro I was just bullshitting, you know we didn't come down here for that. We left the room and headed over to see Big Wayne at Pressure World Car Wash.

We got the ride cleaned up while we got at some of North and South Memphis finest. Two sisters pulled up in an Escalade and I got at the driver. I asked the driver what's yo name and she said Cookie. I released some of that west Nashville swag on her and she was instantly hooked.

Black got at her sister Carmalita and they seemed to hit it off real good. I continued to rap with Cookie because I was feeling her, when she stepped out of the truck I noticed she was six feet or so.

We continued to talk until my ride was ready so I told her to hit me up and we would kick it later. We exchanged numbers then I pulled off heading to the Gucci store to get fresh for the game.

We shopped at the Gucci store and headed back to the hotel to drop our bags off then we headed back out. I was bored so I rode through the short end of Hyde Park, Douglas, Walkins, Brown Dixie Holmes and Cordova.

We looked at houses in German town and I was feeling like I wanted to buy one. We almost got pulled over by the police so I kept it moving.

We drove to the fed ex forum and bought a ticket to the Grizzlies game. Black Obama complained about the tickets. I told him that I should have left his ass in Nashville with all that crying because I came to ball.

We went into the arena and walked around for a minute checking out the building. Black wanted to see the game but I wanted get at some hoes. Everybody was looking good and thick so therefore I was looking for a bitch to fuck cause the blunts had me feeling real freaky.

We went and found our seats then started watching the game. The Grizzlies was balling and the stadium was live. Zach Randolph was killing san Antonio.

Soon as the game was over we asked some people what's popping and they said we are going to a party over on Beal Street. I said hell yea that's what's up Beal, here we come.

We went into BB King Bar and Grill and got some drinks in our system then we headed back outside to hang out. We went from spot to spot for about two hours then we decided to go over to Pure Passion and see some ass and titties.

We made it to the club within ample amount of time. We parked and quickly went in and took a seat close to the stage. We started waving dollars in the girl's direction and instantly we got all of the attention.

The girl onstage stop her dancing and came over and made her ass clap and Black Obama started making it rain.

While he was making it rain I started picking money up off the floor and cuffing it. She stopped dancing and asked me why I was stealing her money.

I told her bitch I ain't took nothing, then I quickly said ole garbage ass bitch you lucky we even spending money on yo stank ass. She got up in my face like she wanted to fight or something so I shoved her whole face with my hand. A couple of guys jumped up and rushed over to us and one nigga said Jones that's my bitch. I said well you need to teach your hoe some manners.

He swung off on me and missed. Black Obama caught him with a right hook and he fell over a table. The other two guys swung and caught me with a hard blow to the nose and head and blood instantly started pouring out of my nose and into my fresh white Gucci shirt.

Black Obama came from behind and stole on one of the dudes and I quickly regained my focus and swung off on the tall nigga that busted my nose. As we slugged it out a few second security came over and grabbed us then threw us out.

Soon as we got to the parking lot we went back to fighting, I dropped the nigga that Black Obama had knocked over the table. I spun around and notice the other two niggas stomping Black Obama.

I ran to the car and got the four nickel out of the stash and let off five rounds. They started scattering after I hit one of them up. The other two took off.

I ran over to Black Obama to see if he was alright and I noticed that his face was fucked up. I helped him up off the ground and he told me that they had kicked his golds out his mouth.

I asked him could he walk and he said yea I think so, he started limping and I told him lets go before the police arrived. Just as I said that I heard the sound of a chopper let loose and Black Obama went down.

I got low and yelled for him but he didn't move nor answer back. I let off the last few shots of my four nickel and reloaded the clip as the thunder from the chopper continued to ring out.

As the nigga busted the chopper I heard him between shots yell out Orange Mound nigga you fucked up now. Soon as the shooting paused I took out full crank towards my Chevy. I let off a few shots and kept running. I heard the sound of the police coming and then I seen the flashing lights.

I tried to toss the gun and make it to the car. The police swarmed in about ten cars deep and order everybody to put their hands up. The Orange Mound nigga dropped the AK 47 and they put their hands in the air.

They slammed all of us to the ground and quickly hand cuffed us. An officer yelled out call the ambulance we have one with multiple gun shots.

As they was putting me in the back of a car I heard another officer say to the other one that had arrived late, we have three black males in custody, one has been fatally shot multiple times with a large caliber hand gun and another black male DOA.

Another officer took pictures of the AK 47 that laid on the ground. Another officer asked what did this guy get shot with? They started looking for the handgun.

It only took them about five minutes before one officer yelled over here I found it. They quickly took pictures of it and bagged it. They took us over to 201 Popular and locked us up. It took an hour or so but they finally book me in and took my fingerprints.

I asked what was I charged with and they officer read off the charges. Disturbing the peace, assault and reckless endangerment. My bond was set at one hundred and fifty thousand dollars.

I sat in the holding cell pissed off. What started off as a good vacation turned out be a super bad day. I sat there until the officers came to get me.

They changed me out of my bloody Gucci outfit and gave me some county jail clothes. They took me to the floor where I would be housed in and threw me in the cell. A guy named Ronnie Woods gave me the name and number to a good bail bonds man and I thanked him. As much as I hated to I had to call Tre'Von and tell him what happened. I dialed his number and it took him a minute to answer but he answered and I was so relieved. I started explaining my whole situation then he finally said damn bro what do you need me to do?

I told him to call the bondman that Ronnie had recommended and I told him to call Glenn Funk and see how much he would take the case for.

Before I could finish telling Tre'Von what I needed him to do the C.O yelled out Winters you have a visitor to see you so step to the front door.

I hung up and went to see what was going on. The officer hand cuffed me and pulled me out the cell and took me down the hall. He turned me over to a black lady and a white man in a suit.

Once we got to where they wanted to take me they sat me down in an interview room. They said you know why you are here? I looked at them like they were stupid.

The black lady gave me her name and said we are with the Memphis Homicide Division and we would like to talk to you. I said I ain't got no rap.

The black lady said your friend got killed and another guy got shot and we know you have answers. I said I ain't got shit. The guy said we know you didn't kill anyone but we know you know who did the shooting. Before I could speak the lady said we have a forty five automatic handgun with your finger prints on it and guess what? The other guy that was shot multiple times got shot with the same gun your prints are on.

She said if you give us the identity of your friends killer then we will see that you get charged with a lesser charge let's say self-defense or even manslaughter if the guy dies. I said I'm sorry but I can't help you. The guy said god dammit your friend got killed and you don't care, you don't want to see his killer get served justice? I said I didn't say I don't care about him getting killed.

She said okay then please take a look at these three pictures and tell me which one was the shooter. I looked at the pictures real good and said I wish I could help you but I don't know.

The male officer said I don't know how you all do it in Nashville but this is Memphis and we. Before he could finish his sentence I said save all of your speech and good cop, bad cop bullshit for the first 48 bullshit. I can't help you so solve your own fucking case.

I'll see to it that you get life in prison, we have your prints on the gun and we have witnesses that said you assaulted a young woman in the club.

I calmly told the detective to put it all in the motion of discover and give it to my lawyer because I didn't have nothing else to say. I ordered them to take me back to my cell.

He snatched me up out of the seat and escorted me out the room and over to another officer. The other officer escorted me back to the floor I was being housed in.

The C.O. opened the cellyport door and told me to enter. Once I entered he removed my handcuffs and then closed the door. I entered my unit and headed to my cell so I could lay back in my bed and think. I climbed up onto the top bunk and laid back. I thought to myself damn I hope Tre'Von hurry his slow ass up and get here.

Chapter 14

I WOKE UP TO the sound of my alarm clock so I already knew what time it was without looking. I quickly got out of bed and got dressed.

I went to the kitchen and prepared myself a light breakfast for the road. I drunk a tall glass of orange juice and headed out the door with a bagel in my hand.

I worked my way through the morning traffic while slowly eating my raisin filled bagel. Once traffic was clear on Loop 440 I was happy to be able to drive like I wanted to.

I pulled up at the academy and parked. I jumped out of the 'burban and quickly walked to the back and pulled out my gym bag full of necessity and threw it over my shoulder.

I entered the academy and gave my name to the young lady at the front desk. She instructed me where to go and who to ask for. I thanked her and proceeded down the hall.

I quickly found the guy I was waiting to see. He asked my name while shaking my hand. I gave him a firm shake and said Tre'Von Lockridge sir.

He asked me a few questions of why I wanted to become a metro police officer and I gave him all of my reasons. He smiled and said well we could certainly use you here if you can make the cut.

I rubbed my hands together and said I sure hope I make the cut because being an officer is what I have been dreaming about since age seven.

He pat me on the shoulder and said here follow me. We went to a class room and he waited on more guys to come in. once the class got almost full he called role and then introduced himself to the entire class.

He gave us some papers to fill out and another set of papers which was a quiz. I quietly filled out my papers and double checked my answers.

Once we were finished he put on a movie and we sat and watched it until it was over. He gave us a homework assignment then he ended the class.

Before we left he announced that the next day would be a full day and be prepared to take a physical examination and physical fitness test.

I left the academy feeling good and happy. As I put my bag in the back of the truck I heard my cell phone ring. I answered it and it was Je'Von asking me have I left Nashville.

I had totally forgotten about his legal troubles so I quickly told him why I hadn't left yet. He was pissed off beyond ever but I had more important matters to handle.

I told him that I would hit the highway in less than thirty minutes. He said that he would call back in one hour so I said okay bro you do that.

He hung up and I drove home to get what was left of my money. I called Black and asked him for the rest of the money I needed. After I assured him Je'Von would give it back to him he told me to stop by and pick it up.

I drove to the eastside and met Black off of Douglas Ave then I jumped on the highway. Once I was on I-40 west I put in my Sade cd and grooved to the music.

Just as Je'Von had promised he called back within an hour. I assured him that I was on the highway headed to Memphis.

We talked until his phone was about ready to hang up. I told him not to worry then the phone hung up. I went back to grooving to the music of Sade. Forty five minutes into the ride the cd was at the end so I popped in Jill Scott and let her take me away.

After I listened to her cd I noticed that I needed gas so I stopped when I got in to Jackson Tennessee and put a hundred in the tank then continued my course. I wanted to hear something different so I changed cds to Trey Songs and rocked out to that the rest of the way to Memphis. From Jackson Tennessee it only took me a little over an hour to reach Memphis.

I quickly found the Shelby county jail on 201 and popular. I went in and asked if they had a Je'Von Winters? The lady looked in the computer and said yes. I asked her how is the process of bail and she gave me a list of bail bonds men.

I dialed one up and told him what I was trying to do. It only took me about an hour to bail him out. As I waited on Je'Von to walk through the door my stomach started growling something serious.

Je'Von called out my name and I looked up and smiled as I stood to hug him. He smiled and hugged me back. I asked him what was all the mess on his shirt and he said it's a long story.

I said well we have at least a three hour drive back to Nashville so you can tell me your long story then. Soon as we walked out of the county jail he removed his shirt and threw it in the trash.

I said why you do that? He said I'm not wearing a bloody shirt. I said blood who blood was it and why it all over your shirt? He said it was my blood and shit got crazy.

I had wanted to stop and get something to eat but soon as I said that Je'Von remember his car was in the police impound. We stopped and got something to eat at Neely's Interstate Bar B que then we asked for directions of how to get to the police impound.

Once we arrived there we paid the fee and they released the car. Je'Von jumped in the car and we headed back to Nashville. I followed him as he took the lead.

Je'Von sped the entire ride home so I did five to ten miles over the speed limit to keep up with him. We got back from Memphis quicker than we were supposed to so I was happy.

Once we were passing through the Bellevue area of Nashville, Je'Von called me and told me to go to the house on 39th. I drove behind him all the way over to 39th.

He ran into the house so I sat in the truck waiting on him to come back out. Ten minutes later he came to the door waving for me to come into the house.

I turned the truck off and headed into the house. He had stacks of money counted out on the living room table. He gave me my money back and thanked me for coming to his aide.

It felt good to hear him thank me for something for a change. So I finally said don't worry about it, that's what brothers are for. I asked him what happened in Memphis and he told me the story step by step.

When he got to the part of Black Obama getting killed my heart sunk deep down into my chest because I felt bad for his mom. I knew that he was her only child and she would be heart broken.

I asked Je'Von what did they charge him with and he said attempt murder, reckless endangerment, disturbing the peace, and assault.

He smiled and said I slapped a bitch and shot her nigga about three or four times. I said Jay those are some serious charges. He said fuck that shit I ain't going back to court.

I said Jay you got to go because I signed my name on the bond and I can't have you jumped bail on my signature because they will give me problems. Before he could speak I said you know I just started the academy today.

He said chill bro that shit ain't about nothing because those niggas ain't going to want to see me in court because they killed Black O. I said the attempted murder charge should get dropped so it will only be the assault and disturbing the peace charge.

I said damn Jay I hope you are right. He rolled up a blunt and I stood up and quickly headed to the door before he lit it up because I didn't want to be around no marijuana smoke.

I stepped out the door and quickly walked to the truck. I turned the ignition on and headed over to meet Black. And thanked him then I headed home.

Soon as I came into the house Cookie asked me where I had been and I gave her a part of the story. She looked like she was concerned for Je'Von so I assured her that he was fine.

She warmed my food up for me and I ate while watching TV. Soon as I finished eating she washed my plate and ran me my bath water.

I stripped down and took me a long hot bubble bath. She came in and gave me a back massage while I soaked in the tub. Once I finished she washed the bath tub out by hand then came and lay beside me in the bed.

Before I could close my eyes good I was asleep without a care in the world. The next morning came and I awoke to the sound of my alarm clock. I got up and got ready for what I assumed would be an intense day of training. I ate breakfast and headed out the door and over to the police academy.

Chapter 15

I WAS HAPPY TO be out of jail so I smoked blunt after blunt in the memory of my dawg Black Obama. I popped the City paper cd in the radio and put it on the song called dope boy swag while I got high as the moon.

I turned up the volume and let the bass from the 15s take me away as I continued to puff on the diesel. After four blunts to the head I decided to jump in the shower to get the jail smell off of me.

I took one of the longest showers ever but when I was finished I felt like a new man. I put on my $485 pair of Robin jeans and matching shirt and my twenty five hundred dollar USDA airforce ones by young Jeezy.

I hit my neck with two shots of Dolce and Gabbana cologne and then stepped outside to see what was going on in the hood. No sooner then I took six steps out of the house I turned around and went right back in to get my Gucci sunglasses and my .40 caliber Glock.

A few hood rats ran up to me and started begging for some money but I wasn't hearing them. One was willing to trick for a hundred but I laughed and kept it moving.

I thought about Black Obamas mom and headed over to her house to give her the news. I knocked on the door and she answered on the forth knock.

I greeted her then started telling her about her son. Before I could get it out she started crying. She told me that her son got killed in Memphis.

I asked her how did she know and she said the Memphis Homicide Department and morgue contacted me. She started crying even harder. I told her that I was sorry for her loss.

She asked me could I help her with some money for the funeral and burial, I said sure as I reached into my pocket. I gave her a five thousand stack and ask is this enough? She hugged me and asked God to bless me. I told her that I was sorry for her loss and turned to walk off.

I walked over to Billie's barbershop on Clifton to hang out with some of the hood niggas. Soon as I approached the crowd I heard them say damn that's fucked up he got killed.

I assumed that they had heard the news about Black O so I said yea man they killed him right in front of me and there was nothing I could do.

Somebody said what you talking about J-Rock? I said Black O they killed him ain't that what yall talking about? They said we talking about lil Bo.

I poured out some liquor for Lil Bo and made a cross with my hands across my chest then kissed my fingers and held them up to God and said R.I.P Bo we miss you. Once I finished everybody were all saying what happened to Black O? I started telling them Black O got shot and now he's dead.

They listened to the news and they was like damn Black Obama is dead. The streets was getting crazy and I knew that it was about to get even crazier.

We all popped open some beer and liquor and we all drank some forties in their memory.

I rolled a big blunt of diesel and started puffing. After three hard pulls I sent it around in rotation until it was all gone. I continued to drink on my old English 800 until it was damn near gone.

Once I got about a quarter bottle empty I poured it out on the curb for my nigga black Obama. I popped open another beer and started guzzling. It didn't take me long to almost empty that one so I repeated the process but this time in the memory of Lil Boe.

After about an hour or so three cars of police rolled through back to back so I decided to keep it moving since I had a Glock on my waist.

I dapped everybody up and walked back over to 39th. Soon as I set foot on 39th I spotted Keisha coming down the street.

She took one look at me and said what's good. As I was walking up to her I smiled a mouth full of gold teeth then said you are.

As we stood face to face she said I smell it so where is it? I quickly said all I got is hard dick and bubble gum and I just ran out of my last piece from where I'm coming from.

She said aw nigga you got jokes, I laughed as I grabbed a handful of my dick. She watched me hold my dick in my hands. I watched her watch me then I said naw I was just playing I got it right here, what you wanna do?

She said stop fucking around and roll it up so we can get right. I quickly said the blunt is a given but I'm trying to get right with you. She tried to go in my pocket and get the weed out but when she reached in my pocket all she felt was a pocket full of dick.

She quickly withdrew her hand and said Jay you are nasty. I pulled the weed from my right pocket and said is this what you looking for?

She smiled and said what you playing for? I hit the alarm on the Chevy and we both got in. I got behind the wheel and she sat on the passenger seat.

I cranked the car up and the sounds of ice cube blasted through the speakers. I threw her the weed in her lap and put the car in gear as I sung along to the song. Keisha got mad because her lil young ass didn't know the song so she changed it. I looked over at her and said girl you crazy or what? Don't fuck with my music.

Before she could speak Trick Daddy song thug Holiday came on and we both started singing along. I looked over at her and smirked because she was too damn fine to be so gutta.

My buzz from the forty ounces had me feeling good and I couldn't wait for Keisha to roll the blunt. I stopped at the store and bought a box of cigarillos and tossed them in her lap.

She wasted no time on tearing the wrapper off the box and started removing the cigar from the box. Keisha Cole I should have cheated came on and I sat back and listened to her blow.

Keisha split the blunt with her fingernails and emptied the tobacco out the window. We pulled back up in front of the house and she started stuffing the blunt.

I watched her lick the blunt as she was attempting to get it to stick together. As I watched her pretty little pink lips and tongue run around the blunt I instantly became hard, so I thought to myself shit I got to get some of this bitch head.

Mario Winans song keep it on the low came on and she went crazy. I took the blunt from here and dried it with my lighter then I fired it up. I took three good pulls of it then I passed it to her.

As I listened to Mario sing I asked Keisha when I beat that pussy is she going to keep it on the low. She continued to hit the blunt as I continued to talk shit.

I reached between her legs and touched her fat pussy and she slapped my hand. I looked at her and yelled pass the blunt since you tripping. She passed the blunt and I took another three pulls.

As she reached for the blunt the song birthday sex came on and she started grinding her ass deep into my seat. I watched her do her thing. Her nipple was poking through her Bebe shirt and I was getting super turned on.

I told her to roll another blunt as I flicked the roach out the window of the car. As she was rolling the blunt I closed my eyes and listened to the new Kelly Rowland song called motivation.

Keisha sparked the next blunt up and we were back in our grove. As I was about to raise the blunt up to my lips the police rode by and looked our way.

I cursed because the car was full of smoke and I was hoping that they didn't stop. It was two white officers in the car so I tried to play it off.

Soon as they got to the top of the street I told Keisha lets go into the house. We quickly jumped out of the car and headed to my house. By the time we were on the porch and heading into the house the police rode back by.

I peeped through the blinds to see if they stopped. I didn't see them so I told Keisha to light the blunt back up. She lit it back up and we started smoking.

The blunt had me feeling good so I just laid back and zoned out. I began to get the munchies so I went into the kitchen and got some snacks for Keisha and me.

Keisha wanted to watch a movie so I put a porno in by Pinky. She quickly yelled out this ain't no damn movie it's a porno. I said I ain't got no movies, all I watch is porno. I said you want to watch it or not?

We started watching it and instantly the tension started building between the both of us. Pinky started fucking the bitch in the movie with a strap on and my eyes was glued to the screen.

Keisha started complaining about she didn't want to see that shit so I changed the DVD to the Mr. Marcus and Superhead disc. She started talking shit about how Marcus couldn't handle Superhead and I jumped in and said no bitch would ever break me down.

Before I could get past the first scene she was unzipping my pants and pulling me out. She didn't waste no time going down on me. I watched my whole entire dick disappear down her throat.

I pulled my shirt off and came out of my pants. She instantly started rubbing and kissing on my six pack. After she told me that I was fine she went right back to giving me head.

I lay back and watched her deep throat me for about five minutes. I thought to myself you're head is good but you ain't no super head. I was bored with that so I told her to come out of her clothes.

She came out of her clothes and I told her to bend over. She bent over and grabbed her ankles and told me to come and get it. I went straight in with no hesitation.

Her pussy was wet, tight and super-hot. I fucked her Mr. Marcus style about twenty minutes then I got tired so I told her to get on the floor.

I went back on her from the back and she started throwing the pussy to me. She became wetter and wetter and I loved every minute of it. As I was thinking how good her pussy was she started cumming all over my dick.

My knees were starting to burn from the carpet so I started stroking deeper into her pussy as far as I could go. Soon as I was about to cum she made her pussy muscles grip around my dick.

I instantly busted off deep within her. I fell over on top of her and continued pumping until I slide out. I bit her on the back of the neck and whispered in her ear "damn bitch yo pussy is so good"

She got cocky and said yea I know. So I said bitch shut up and roll another blunt. She rolled over and asked for the weed. I grabbed it off the table and threw it at her.

We smoked another blunt together and fell asleep. When I woke up she was gone and so was all the money in my pocket. I swore to slap the shit out of her the next time I saw her.

I jumped up and went to the shower because I had dried up pussy juices all over me. I wasn't in the shower a good ten minutes when I got a call from Lil Wendell.

He was letting me know that Rome was over Stacy's house getting his freak on. I said yea okay thanks for the info. I quickly jumped out of the shower and got dressed into all black Gucci outfit.

I grabbed the Remington 308 sniper rifle and headed out the back door. I crept through the neighborhood until I had finally got to the section were Stacy lived.

Only a few people was out on that end of the hood so I wasn't worried about being spotted. I found me a nice size rock and scooped it up then threw it as hard as I could at Rome's car window.

Instantly the window shatters and the car alarm went crazy. I quickly crouched into the bushes and waited. As I jumped into the bush I noticed the two girls and guy on the corner glance over towards the car but they didn't pay it no mind because no one was out to be seen. I looked back towards Stacy's front door and shortly after Rome came running out with his pistol in hand.

He ran up to his car and pointed the gun into the busted window but no one was there. He swirled around pointing the pistol in nothing but air.

I watched him from the bushes as he looked under the car. Stacy was looking out her bedroom window as he yelled to her to get him a trash bag and some tape.

Soon as she disappeared from the window I hit him with the 308 from inside the bush. Before the shot sounded off he was already hitting the ground and I was running full crank in the other direction.

It took me five minutes to make it back to the house. I put the gun into the project dumpster and kept moving. I went to the trunk of my car and made a cocktail then lit it and threw it in the same dumpster that I had dumped the gun in.

Instantly the dumpster went up in a blaze and I headed back to my car and fled the scene. I went and got me a hotel room at the Double tree and laid back.

After my second day of laying low that's when it hit me. I went to the bathroom to take a piss and my dick was on fire, it felt like I was pissing razorblades.

I looked at the inside of my boxers and I noticed all of the nasty yellow greenish shit on them. I cursed a few times and squeezed my dick a few times in hopes of stopping my piss from coming out.

I quickly washed up and changed underwear then headed to Lentz Health Clinic. I had to sit over there about four hours before someone finally called my name.

The doctor asked me to come to the back. He read the paper that I filled out then he told me to pull my pants down. I dropped my pants to the floor and the doctor put his gloves on.

He pulled out a long metal rod device and carefully stuck it up the shaft of my dick. Instantly tears came out my eyes and I screamed like a bitch.

As he was removing the device it started hurting even more so I closed my eyes and gritted my teeth together. He told me that he would be right back so sit still and be patient.

When he returned he told me Mr. Winters you have a bad case of gonorrhea. He said I'm going to prescribe you some antibiotics called penicillin you should take one capsule twice a day until your bottle is empty.

I said okay that sound good. He said make sure you take them on a full stomach. I said okay. He then asked me did I know the name of the person who I had unprotected sex with.

I told him that her name is Stacy and he said Stacy who? I didn't even know her last name so I simply said I can't remember. He told me that it was important to remember because she needs to come in and get tested.

I told him that I would tell her if I see her again. He said not to be having unprotected sex and handed me the prescription. I thanked him and quickly headed out of the clinic before somebody noticed me and put my business all through the hood.

I headed straight to Walgreens and got my prescription filled because it hurt like hell everytime I had to piss. I swore to myself that soon as I saw Keisha lil dirty pussy ass again I would slap the piss out of her lil dick sucking ass.

I answered my phone and Lil Wendell was telling me that I was a beast. I knew what he was talking about so I started laughing. We joked around for a few minutes then I hung up.

As I was coming out of the Walgreens I spotted JBo baby momma and I thought back how good her pussy was when I took it on the home invasion.

I walked up to her and spoke. She waved and said hey so I asked her what is your name? She smiled and said Niecy. I said damn shawty you look good do you have a man. Me knowing damn well what the answer was but I waited on the response.

She said no I'm single right now. I said what's a fine thing like you doing single? She said it's a long and complicated story that's hard to discuss.

I said oh I'm sorry if I'm being nosey but would it be okay if I take you out for dinner? She said I don't know about that. I said why not.

She said well for starters you haven't even told me your name. I said my name is Je'Von. She said well Je'Von that sounds nice but I think I'ma have to pass.

I said can we at least be friends, allow me to give you my number that way we can get to know each other a little better and you will feel more comfortable when I ask to take you out again.

She looked at me like maybe she knew who I was then after a long ten seconds of quietness she finally said okay I guess I could use a friend. We exchanged numbers then I watched her walk off.

As she headed to the car I was hypnotized from her sexy walk and fat ass. She was a brick house to be as short as she was, I was lusting so hard that I didn't even realize I had started grabbing my crouch.

I snapped out of my thoughts and headed back to my whip. I stopped at Burger King and got me a number one combo with cheese then I headed back to the hood.

Once I reached the Jungle I parked and started eating my food half way through my meal I decided to take the penicillin because I was tired of my dick burning.

The vice was riding through the jungle almost every twenty minutes or so I decided to keep it moving. I rode over to the Antioch area to see if I could catch the nigga Eric.

I posted up across the street from his warehouse about two hours. I started to get bored so I decided to move on. I went over to the eastside to holla at Black.

We discussed some business then I decided to head back out west. Once out west I bought a few tabs from Do-Bug then headed over to Obama market to get a Arizona tea.

I caught a few sells then headed to freaky Teresa house to see who all was over there. She wasn't at home so I headed back to 39th and chilled because my pills kicked in and I was feeling real good.

Chapter 16

POLICE ACADEMY WAS FUN and exciting, every day I was learning new things about being an officer and I was happy as can be. On top of that my moms had got approved for the house and all I had to do was help her move all of her furniture in.

Cookie and I were now married and life was great. I felt like I had the whole world in my hands. Soon as I got out from the academy I headed over to Wal-Mart and picked up the photos from the wedding.

I sat in the truck and looked at them and smiled to myself. Cookie and I looked great as a couple and I was happy that we went ahead and tied the knot.

When I got to my mom's, Je'Von, Jonathon, and I were clowning around. I smiled even harder because I couldn't believe Je'Von came and showed his support.

I put the photos away and started the truck up. I went to get my mom so we could do the furniture moving. Soon as I arrived at her house she wasted no time with the packing.

We started grabbing all the small stuff that would fit in the suburban and we headed over to the U-Haul company. I picked out a medium large truck, paid cash and we exited the lot.

Once back at mom's house I paid some crackheads twenty dollars a piece to help me load up all the furniture into the truck. It took us about an hour but we had finally loaded up everything my moms wanted to take.

Before we left I called Je'Von up because he didn't want nobody going in his room touching nothing. He said that he would move his own stuff so we locked the spot up and took off to the new house.

Once we arrived at the new house I took my time unloading everything because I didn't have the help that I needed. My mom was so happy and I was happy for her because it was her first house.

I thought to myself just as soon as I graduate police academy and I become an officer I can save up some money and Cookie and I will be able to get our new house.

My mind drifted off to Cookie and the wonderful sex, it seemed like the sex was getting better and better since I said "I do".

I snapped out of my thoughts when I heard my moms call my name. She asked me was I going to finish helping her unload the truck; I smiled and said yea ma I got you.

I went back to unloading the truck with my mom until it was all unloaded. She said she would organize it all later so I said cool then we headed back out west.

Since Je'Von was going to take care of his own room I decided to take the U-Haul truck back to the store. Moms followed me there and I turned it in.

We stopped at Applebee's and had dinner together then it was time for me to head home and help Cookie pack for our weekend trip. Once I was at home I helped her with the luggage.

Soon as everything was packed we jumped on highway I-24 and headed to the A. The drive was nice and short so we got there in less than two and a half hours.

We grabbed us a hotel room unloaded the bags then headed right back out to see the town. Once in the car I turned the CD player off and turned to Hot 107.9.

We roll over Piedmont Park to see what was cracking. After leaving the park we decided to go ahead and do some shopping so we stopped at the store called Seven over at Escape and Adidas at Lenox. Cookie wanted something out of J. Crew and the Michael Kors store.

Upon leaving the mall we drove around down town Atlanta just to doing some sight seeing then Cookie decided that she wanted to go in the beauty salon calledTag Concept so we stopped by and went in. as we was getting out of the car I was telling her that she probably wouldn't be able to just walk in an get a chair because they were probably all booked up.

Just as I thought every chair and hair station was full. We left there and went to another salon called the j-Spot and it was just as Tag Concept.

I assured her that her hair was fine and we headed back to the car. She gave me a kiss then thanked me. Since we were still on Peachtree road we decided to also eat on Peachtree.

Cookie wanted to eat at justin's and I wanted to eat at Houston's, since we couldn't agree with one another we decided to try out the restaurant called The Oceanaire.

The restaurant was very nice looking and comfortable, we sat down and ordered from the menu. Right away I noticed that the prices weren't cheap but it didn't matter.

We sat and ate a very delicious meal that was well worth the money then we left. I drove around until we were on Caroline Street so we stopped at sole to do some more shopping.

Before I left Sole I asked the guy at the counter what club was jumping tonight. He said that I should go to Esso on 1599 Memorial Drive.

I thanked him and headed out with Cookie. Once we got into the car I told her listen, During the day we will visit different spots of the city and at night we will do a different night club every night.

Since she hadn't been to a strip club I agreed to take her to one. She wanted to go to Magic City but I told her Magic City is best on Mondays and since we would be gone come Monday we would miss out.

I told her how about Esso tonight, 112 or Strokers on Saturday, and The Velvet Room on Sunday. She said that sounded like a plan so we headed back to our hotel room to put our bags up and change our clothes.

It seemed like it took Cookie forever to get dressed but once she did come out the bathroom she was gorgeous. I have never seen her all dressed up with makeup on except at the wedding and that didn't count because she had on a wedding dress.

Seeing her in a short skirt with heels on made her body look amazing, the three inch heels made her calves and ass look extremely good. I complimented her style of dressing then we headed out to the club.

Once at the club the music was pumping and the drinks were flowing. We ordered a few drinks to get us started then we sat back and enjoyed ourselves.

The club was full of beautiful model looking chicks and a lot of wanna-be-ballers. Cookie was ordering Ciroc and cranberry juice and drinking it like it was water.

About the time I realized it she was already on her third one. I attempted to slow her down because the drink had her feeling good. She wanted to make love in the club with everyone watching.

I told her to chill and behave but she just kept getting naughty. She reached under the table and started fondling my dick while she sucked on my right earlobe.

A bad yellow bone chick kept giving me the eye and I looked away every time. Five minutes later I had to go to the bathroom to release my liquor. As I came back to my table I noticed the girl that was flirting with me sitting at the table with Cookie. The closer I got to the table she was looking more and more like the rapper Trina.

Her and Cookie were laughing and talking so I politely tapped her on her shoulder and said excuse me but do I know you.

She introduced herself as Rita and asked me if I was interested in having a three some. I looked at cookie and she said baby let's do it sounds like it might be fun.

As fine as she was I didn't have a problem with it as long as cookie was down so I thought about it quickly and said okay let's do it.

I ordered another patron for me and a peach Ciroc for Rita then we all left. We went back to our hotel room and the party began. As I entered the room I thought to myself damn I'm the luckiest man alive.

A threesome with my Korean wife and a sexy thick yellow bone looking broad, I pinched myself to make sure it wasn't a dream. As my arm stung from the pinch, I started removing my clothes.

I helped Rita out of her clothes and she helped Cookie out of her skirt and top. Rita didn't waste any time in kissing on my abs and sucking on the head of my already swollen dick.

Cookie joined in and they both took turns sucking on a different body part until they both was down to my balls. Rita sucked on one while Cookie sucked on the other.

At the same time both of them started licking each side of my dick and I was trying not to lose the war that was brewing deep inside me.

Moments later I exploded all over Cookies face and without hesitation Rita licked all of my juices from Cookies face. Rita laid Cookie down on the bed and started gently licking between Cookie thighs until cookie was begging for it.

She then started sucking on Cookies clit. I sat back and watched because I was enjoying the show. Three minutes of watching and listening to the sounds of Rita slurping on cookies juicy wet pussy and I was back hard.

I put on a condom and entered Rita from the back while she continued to eat Cookie up. Rita pussy was tight like fish pussy so I had to talk dirty as I stroked it.

The wetter she became the deeper I went until she was moaning in pure ecstasy. I deep stroked long and hard and fast and she started gripping the sheets.

Cookie was starting to feel left out because Rita had stopped sucking on her due to the serious pounding she was taking. I stopped my stroke and told them lets change positions.

I lay on my back and told Cookie to ride my face while Rita rode my dick reverse cowgirl. Cookie jumped on my face and quickly started grinding while Rita continued to ride my dick like a cowgirl in a horse riding movie.

Cookie came first then Rita. I was harder than penitentiary steel and I wasn't stopping until I bust a hole in something or until I explode again.

Once Rita came she couldn't take the entire dick that I was delivering so she got off and Cookie removed the condom and jumped on. I continued to drill cookie long deep and hard until finally I release my load deep inside her.

Rita started licking Cookie's juices from off my face like a cat cleans itself and Cookie wanted to taste herself off my dick. I laid there while they both cleaned me up from different ends. I was spent but cookie wanted me to give her more. Rita lay beside me with her head on my stomach and Cookie started stroking my dick in hopes of getting it back up.

After five minutes she got mad and gave up. Rita asked could she take a shower so I said of course while pointing towards the shower.

Cookie was looking like she wanted to fight so I decided to give her some head while Rita was showering. It didn't take Cookie five minutes of receiving my tongue and she was already cumming again.

I started licking her ass and she went straight into multiple orgasms. By the time Rita came out of the shower and got dressed Cookie had busted three nuts and she was totally happy.

Rita thanked us for the excitement then headed towards the door. I hated to see her sexy ass leave but I was sure glad she came.

Cookie caught me staring at her fat ass as she was leaving. Once Rita was gone Cookie said babe you like her ass? I said what? She said I know you like her ass cause you couldn't stop looking.

Before I could speak she said you want my ass to look like that? I laughed and said baby no, you are straight just the way you are. She said I don't believe you. I said baby you good so don't trip. She said give me an ass like that. I said what? She said fuck me in my ass so it can be like hers. I said girl you are crazy as I couldn't stop from laughing.

I saw she was serious so I stopped laughing and said okay baby we will work on it. She said lets start right now. She started licking the head of my dick like an ice cream cone and instantly my dick started rising like a cobra.

Soon as I was rock hard I wasted no time bending her over. I went straight in her dripping wet pussy to lube myself up real good then after a few strokes I took my time in entering her tight hot ass.

Before I could get a quarter of the way past the head she was already starting to crawl away from me. I pinned her neck and head down on the bed and continued to ease deeper inside her.

She started whining while speaking Korean but I kept going until I was completely lost inside of her. She said it felt like her ass was going to explode and I pulled out of her and spit on my dick until I was lubed up some more.

Her ass was tighter than a noose around a slave's neck and I could feel her ass muscle contracting all over my swollen hard dick. I took my time until she loosened up then I gave her what she thought she wanted.

She cried blood sweat tears as I stroked deep within her ass. I slapped pulled squeezed and pounded her ass until it was red sore and hurting.

Once I finally finished she went straight to sleep and I headed to the shower to wash off. The next morning she couldn't get out of bed so I went and got us some breakfast at McDonalds.

She ate while lying on her stomach so I decided to cuddle with her while I searched through the cable channels. Once it was noon I was ready to go out and see the city but she said her ass was hurting and she also had a hangover.

I went back out to get her some Aleve for her headache. I rode through Piedmont Park and watched the people hangout. Then I rode by Clark University to see what was happening.

After that I headed back to the room to give her the Aleve, she was sleep so I left the pills and wrote a note then I headed back out. I decided to stop at the underground to see what was jumping off. I only stayed there about an hour then headed over to the store called envy on Euclid Avenue. From there I stopped in at Good Fellaz barbershop and got my hairline edged up and my beard trimmed.

After that I decided to go back and check on Cookie at the hotel. Soon as I stepped back into the door she said that she was just about to call me.

We laid around and cuddled while we watched movie after movie. After the third one we headed over to Justin's and got something to eat. I was happy that she was feeling better so I asked her did she still wanted to go to Club 112.

We got dressed then we headed out to the club. Once we got there I told Cookie to let's get a seat up front. It was crowded but we found a good seat and started watching the show.

We ordered a few drinks and kicked back, Cookie decided to buy me a lap dance because she wanted to see how I was going to act. I got a dance from a thick chocolate stallion that stood about 5'9.

She wasted no time in put it all in my face and getting up close and personal. Once she bent over and started making her ass cheeks clap one at a time I became tuned in.

Cookie watched in great amazement because she had never seen anything quite like that before. Once the dance was over I gave her a tip and thanked her. She went on her way and I ordered another drink because I was fired up and ready to party.

I wasn't in the club forty minutes and a lot of commotion broke out. Waka Flocka Flame and his boys came in and started making it rain and the club went wild.

The DJ pumped his song "itsz a party" and money continued to fly everywhere. Since I didn't have money to blow I stood back and watched all the girls shake it and take it off.

Drinks were plentiful for everyone and the excitement level was high. Each girl in the club was trying to outdo the next and Waka Flocka and his crew kept throwing money like it was candy.

I pulled out my camera phone and started taking pictures because I knew that no one back home would believe me. I must have taken over a hundred or so pictures because I ran out of memory on my phone so I deleted a few text messages.

Cookie had started to feel left out so she was ready to go. I pleaded with her to stay but she insisted that the strip club thang was not for her, so we left there and headed back to the room.

Once back at the hotel we showered and laid back for a while. She wanted to read her book For the taste of sex" by Mr. Mafia so I decided to log on to Facebook and upload some of the club pictures.

Once cookie started reading her book she quickly became horny so she wanted to have sex. I logged out of Facebook and happily gave her what she wanted. After forty five minutes or so of hot and sweaty sex, we both fell into a deep sleep.

The next morning we woke up to a nice day with clear skies so we decided to catch a Braves baseball game. We drove over to the stadium parked and went in.

Since we were a little early we got some good seats. I wanted to see everything that I could possibly see so I didn't waste any time in calling a vendors over to me so I could get food and drinks for me and Cookie.

The white guy that was sitting next to me leaned over and started telling me to watch out for Jurrgen, the pitcher. I asked him who did Jurrgen pitch for and he told me Atlanta.

Soon as the game came on Cookie was on her feet cheering and enjoying herself. I sat back and ate my hot dog thinking to myself damn when the action going to start.

I thought that it would be a lot of excitement since Atlanta was playing St. Louis but to my surprise Jurrgen turned out to be a pretty good pitcher for Atlanta.

By the time the game reached the bottom of the seventh ending I was bored and ready to go because the score was only two and two.

I had ate two hot dogs and drunk two sodas already and I was still hungry so I told Cookie lets go and grab something to eat at Houston's restaurant.

She didn't want to go but quickly gave in and said okay babe lets go. We gathered up our camera and iPods then left. Once at Houston's we sat down to a good meal that was way better than some hot dogs.

I ate my meal and thought about how I would miss going to the velvet room but I knew that we had to get back to Nashville. After we finished our meal we headed back to the hotel to relax and spent some quality time with one another.

After a good hour of relaxing I was dosing off because the meal I had eaten was heavy on my stomach. Around seven p.m Cookie woke me up and asked was I ready to hit the road.

I got up and got myself together then I helped her pack our bags and we checked out. Since I was feeling refreshed from my nap I decided to drive.

I set the iPod on Usher and hit the highway heading home to Nashville, Tennessee. The drive was only a quick three hour ride so I reached the crib in no time at all.

I helped Cookie with all of the bags that we had then went straight to the shower. She came in then we showered together and passionately kissed and caressed one another until I was unbelievably hard.

We exited the shower and headed straight to the bedroom. I didn't waste any time spreading her legs and helping myself to a mouthful of sweet Asian pussy.

She moaned and spoke Korean as I buried my tongue deep down within her. By the time I started sucking on her swollen clit she had started to talk dirty.

Her pussy started pulsating and I knew it wouldn't be long before she blew her load all over my face. As I sucked on her clit I kept my eyes on her stomach. Soon as her stomach started shaking I knew she was ready. I applied more pressure to her clit and with the snap of a finger she came all over my face. I continued sucking and licking as she fought to catch her breath. Her face was bright red and her pussy pulsated nonstop as I continued to suck her dry.

I pushed her legs up towards the ceiling and climbed between them and inserted a stiff ten inches of rock hard lean dick. She begged for me to fuck her and I gave her just what she wanted.

Three minutes later she was biting down on my neck as she started to have multiple orgasms. I pulled out to let her taste the dick.

She happily started giving me some head until I was trying to pull away. She tightened her mouth around my dick and sucked hard as she could a few times and I shot a load of cum deep within her mouth and throat.

As I was cumming she started beating my dick on her face as she continued to stroke it with her hands. Instantly her face became covered with cum but she continued on until I was hard again.

Once I was hard again she started sucking my cum covered nuts until I couldn't take it any longer. I turned her over on her stomach and entered her from the back.

Right around the time I came deep within her, she was also cumming. I laid down on top of her dripping in sweat as we both fought to catch our breath. We laid in a spoon position as I kissed on her neck and earlobe. Twenty minutes later I fell into a deep sleep.

Chapter 17

I WAS NOW KICKING it with Niecy on a daily basis and I was finding out that she was a cool person. At first I thought she was just another hood rat with a super fat ass, but I quickly started to see that she wasn't.

What I liked about her most she is a hard worker with plenty of motivation and drive. Her credit was A-1 and she's a totally independent woman.

She slowly started telling me about her past and her plans for the future. And I was all ears because I had never met a woman like her before.

Our sex life was great and I was fighting for control of my emotions, because she was a lady in the streets but a complete animal in bed. My mind was blown from her skills and techniques that I was starting to fall in love.

I now had my own key to her house and I was sleeping over at least three nights a week. During the day time I would hustle hard and during the night I would spend quality time with her and her daughter.

Her cooking reminded me of my mom's cooking so I ate everything she cooked. It took me a couple months to realize that my face was getting fat and my stomach was starting to poke out of my shirt.

I made a mental note to myself to start working out but between hustling and spending time with Niecy I hadn't had a chance to actually make it to the gym.

As I lay comfortably in the bed with Niecy I waited on my phone to ring so I could sell the last few ounces of coke that I had remaining. My phone wasn't ringing quickly enough so I decided to head over to rabbit house and see what was happening in the trap.

I got dressed and headed over there with no delay. Soon as I arrived there I asked Rabbit who needed something. He told me that business was slow because lil Bud had the best prices in the hood and everyone was copping from him.

I decided to do something about that so I headed back home and got my Glock 40 with the extended clip and went looking for him. I hung out on the block for a few hours until I realized that I wasn't going to run into him no time soon.

I decided to drive off to the North side and see what was shaking. I pulled up on Delk Avenue and caught a few heads spending ten dollars apiece.

I served them all and collected my money. I kept it moving until I was in Dodge City projects. I quickly rode through without stopping then I headed over to T and T car wash to get my Chevy cleaned up. I pulled in and hopped out of the car, I tossed the worker the keys and let him pull my car into the spot where he wanted my car to be situated and parked.

As my car got washed my ex-Westside homie Tim Low pulled up and came over to holla at me. He wanted to know what I was letting my quarter keys go for so I told him ten grand even.

He said that he would hit me up for a quarter later if I would bring it out to the Bordeaux area. I told him that I would bring it and he said cool.

I gave him my number and he pulled off like a bat out of hell. It only took about twenty minutes for my car to get washed and vacuumed out so I paid and left as quickly as I came. I decided to drive over to the eastside to see what was cracking in Shepard wood. Soon as I got there the sales was booming so I decided to get me a piece of the pie.

It only took me an hour or so to sell everything I had so I was all smiles when I ran out of crack. Just as I was finished serving a tall chick named Shaker tried to holla at me.

I stopped and listened to what she had to say. She wanted to hook up with me so I gave her my number and told her to hit me up. Soon as I handed her my number two young niggas started screaming some rah rah shit about I'm out of bound.

I quickly told Shaker to call me later and noted that she should leave before trouble popped off. She took off in the other direction as I started heading for my car.

One of the young niggas picked up a stick and the other had a knife in his hand that looked like a baby machete. I started sprinting toward the Chevy in hopes of getting my strap.

Once at the car I quickly got the Glock 40 out from under the seat and let off about ten shots. Both of them took for cover behind a parked car.

I was about to keep busting my gun but stopped as I noticed a black escalade ride through that fitted the description of who I was looking for.

I jumped into my car and quickly started it up in hopes of catching up with the truck. I made a U-Turn in the middle of the street of Sheppard wood. I had easy caught up to the truck as it was turning the corner. I slowed down to keep my distance as I followed it to a house over behind Pama-Rama apartments.

I pulled in and waited at Pama-Rama until the occupant of the truck was ready to leave again. I made a mental note of which house he went in as I patiently waited for him to come out.

He was only there ten minutes or so then he was back in traffic. I made sure I stayed three or four cars back as I tailed him. He drove through different areas of the city then he finally made the stop that I was hoping for.

I watched the truck drive up to the storage warehouse complex that I had been scoping out. He pulled up to the security booth flashed something to the security guard then was permitted into the gate.

I watched to see which storage area he went to. I started putting the storage number into my phone so I wouldn't forget anything.

I watched him take a Louis Vuitton duffle bag into the storage and and come back out with a big gym bag. He jumped into the truck and quickly headed out of the complex.

I jumped in traffic behind him and followed him through south Nashville and Antioch. He made stops after stops until he finally decided to go home.

I watched him pull up to the security gate in his gated community. He pressed his code into the gate and it quickly opened and shut behind him.

I smiled to myself as I made a u turn and drove off with one thing on my mind. I fired up a blunt of purple haze and popped the Lil Wayne mix cd into the radio.

Soon as Lil Wayne went off I popped that Rick Ross rich forever cd in and headed to the jungle on the Westside.

Niggas and bitches was everywhere and plenty of money was coming through. Do Bug quickly told me that the work was drying up in the streets.

I spoke with him for a moment then I hollered at Chip and Naris before I sped off to 43rd and on to Tennessee Village.

I stopped in Tennessee Village and bought me two Lortabs then I headed back over to 39th. Once I got by Billy's barbershop I had to go the back way because Generation X was filming a video.

I drove up to the house and got my plan together of how I was going to get into the storage. While I was deep in thought Tre'Von called me asked to borrow some money.

I wanted to tell him hell no then I quickly got the idea of the century. I told Tre'Von I needed his help with something.

He asked what did I need help with and I asked him to stop by the house so we could discuss it face to face.

When he got there I offered him something to drink and he said a glass of Kool-Aid. I went into the kitchen and poured him a medium glass of Kool-Aid then I dropped the Lortab into his drink.

When I returned with the drink I patiently waited on him to drink it all down. As he drunk his drink he started to tell me what he needed the money for.

About the time the pill kicked in I put my plan into action. I got Tre'Von to tell me where his keys were to his police car.

Once I got his keys he gave me directions to his house so I quickly drove to his place. Upon entering his apartment I searched through his closet until I found his uniform.

I put on his police uniform and headed out the door with a smile on my face. He followed behind me repeatedly asking me what I was doing.

I got behind the wheel of the car and he jumped in the passenger side. I drove until I came upon the storage building that I was looking for.

I pulled to the gate the security guard asked me how can I help you? I told him which storage I wanted to search.

He asked me where the search warrant was so I got a little slick with him and showed him my badge and said here go your damn search warrant buddy.

He refused to cooperate until he called his manager so I had to think quick before he dialed his manager. Without thinking I took out the Glock 40 with the silencer and shot him twice between the eyes.

Tre'Von was hesitant, I quickly told Tre'Von to help me get his fat ass into the trunk. Tre'Von stared while shaking his head no no no.

Tre'Von grabbed his feet and I grabbed his arms and we proceeded to put him in the trunk of the police car.

Blood was everywhere but the mission had to be completed. Once we dumped his fat ass in the trunk we headed straight up to the storage area.

I didn't waste any time breaking into it so I could get what I came for. Tre'Von stayed in the car listening to the radio because he wanted to make sure the cops weren't somehow called.

Once into the storage department I quickly noticed an old school Chevy and a lot of nice furniture. I went to the car first and attempted to open the door but it was locked.

I stuffed the Glock into my pants and use the box cutters to break out the driver said window. I opened the door and leaned in attempting to pop the trunk from the glove compartment but it wouldn't open.

I quickly went to the trunk pulled out the Glock let out a few rounds until it came open.

My eyes lit up when I saw the two Louis Vuitton luggage bags; I grabbed the bags and started to open them. Bingo it was what I was hoping for.

I quickly opened the second bag and smiled even harder. I started transferring some of the money from one suit case to the other because I planned on giving Tre'Von the one with the lesser amount.

Once the transfer was complete I started searching through the dressers and the other furniture. Jack pot I was having a wonderful day. I found two trash bags, one full of molly pills and Lortabs and the other trash bag was bricks of coke.

I called Tre'Von to come and help me so we could get the hell up out of there. We pulled the security guard out of the trunk and replaced him with the money and drugs then we were back into traffic like nothing had happened.

I drove back to Tre'Von's house because I didn't want to pull up on 39th in the police car.

Once inside of Tre'Von's apartment I quickly remembered that I had shortened the money from one bag so I quickly gave it to him and told him whatever is in it is all yours.

He opened it and was very happy with what he saw. I didn't open my bag because it was busting out of the seams with money.

I quickly brought his attention to the pills and coke because I knew he probably wouldn't want anything to do with it.

I asked him what did he want to do about the pills and coke and to my surprise he suggested that we split them up 50/50.

I wanted to put a bullet in his greedy ass for even suggesting something like that but I quickly let it go and simply said okay bro lets count em out as I was pointing at the bricks.

It was a total of ten bricks in the bag so we split em up 5 and 5. I was hoping that I could somehow get Tre'Von five because coke was selling at an all-time high since the drought had hit.

Looking at the four zip lock bags of pills I didn't want to count each pill so I just gave Tre'Von one bag of molly's and 1 bag of Lortabs and we called it even.

Since Tre'Von was the police I knew he couldn't sell his share of the dope so I asked him what he planned to do with it.

He said he would hold it until he figured out what he was going to do with it. I offered to buy his shared and he asked how much.

I was boiling hot but I played it cool and said okay lil bro just let me know what your price is and we will work it out.

Soon as I left his house I started plotting on how I would get his share. I headed to west Nashville and flooded the jungle with the five thousand tabs that I had.

I broke my five bricks down into ounces and started selling them for twelve hundred each. A few niggas wanted to buy some weight but I quickly told them hell no.

I quickly made it known that I had to have the strength for the coke but I was giving deals on the pills.

Niggas like Lil Bud, Ovadue, Chip and Bug lined up for the pill deals while other niggas argued over coke prices.

Twenty minutes of hanging out in the jungle had made me a quick thirty grand so I walked around to Billy's Barbershop and let Mike-Mike trim my beard.

As I was in the barbershop getting my beard trimmed the news came on and it was showing the bloody body of the security guard in the storage.

Mike cut the volume up and we listened in. The police chief spoke of the crime and asked for any witnesses to come forth then he announced that the owner of the storage compartment was the only suspect arrested for questioning.

Of course that news was the talk of the barbershop for twenty minutes or so then everybody went back to what they was doing.

Three day later I was out of pills and coke so I was getting desperate to get what Tre'Von had. I called him up and made him an offer of one hundred racks for his five bricks and ten thousand pills.

He gladly accepted the offer and I was happy I didn't have to rob him for it. I took him the money and we made the exchange.

He was happy to get the money and I was happy to get the dope at such a cheap price. Selling the ounces at 12 a piece I would make two hundred and eleven racks just off of the coke.

I smiled because that wasn't even including the five thousand molly's and the five thousand tabs.

I gave Tre'Von the money and quickly headed back out west to the jungle to get off what I had.

When I pulled up young Buck and City Paper was shooting a video for their G.A.S 2 mix tape cd. T Hyde and D-Strap had their Generation X tee shirts on and the rest of West Nashville had their R.I.P Lil Bo and Dream Team-Lil Donnie Fly tee shirts on.

I brought a blunt of loud from Buck and kept it moving. It was money to get and I wanted it all.

I took care of everybody out west then hit the north side, once night fell I decided to go down Donks sports bar and grill to unwind a lil bit.

Once at Donk's, it was on and popping I had about six drinks and got loose. I watch Marisol and Nunu do their thing.

Ass was everywhere and I was loving it. I ordered a plate of hot wings and told them let the drinks keep coming because the bar was on me.

Around three that morning I left with Marisol and we headed to the room. She was on her bars and I was on my tabs and Ciroc.

Around noon I woke up head spinning. I showered and left her there sleeping with a wet ass. I went home and got myself together then hit up the restaurant called the Grill at Green Hills.

After eating there I went over to Green Hills mall and shopped out at the Louis Vuitton, Gucci, and Nordstrom stores.

My cheapest outfit was true religion and my cheapest watch was a Hublot black caviar band. I bought about eight pair of retro Jordan's for a buck eighty a piece to make my everyday outfits complete then I was back to the hood.

Later that night I went to the whiskey kitchen to have a few drinks then I headed out to Club Ciroc to release my dope boy swag on them.

I was Gucci down from head to toe. The Hublot was like a hundred degree sun on my wrist every time the light hit it.

All eyes were really on me but I didn't give a fuck because I had the Glock 40 on my side and a chopper in the car.

While in the club I was approached by a thick brown skinned girl named Tangie. She whispered in my ear "would you like to have a three some with me and my bitch?"

My dick instantly got hard and I smiled while shaking my head yes. She walked over to her girl and said something then they both headed back my way.

I followed them out the club and we wasted no time getting to our cars. Once at my car I told her that I would follow her. She told me that she was heading to her house in Smyrna, Tennessee.

I said cool and started the car up. It only took us about 15 minutes to get there but the whole entire drive I was in my rearview checking for the set up.

We pulled up to her house and quickly went in. I didn't waste no time in locking the door behind me as I entered.

They lead me to the bedroom and I started removing my clothes. Tangie's girlfriend started eating her pussy quicker than I could get undressed.

While they were occupied I quickly slide the Glock 40 between my shirt and pants so they wouldn't see it.

I watched them eat each other for a few minutes then I went over to get some head from Tangie. As she started deep throating me and licking my balls, her girl got a lil upset so Tangie stopped.

Tangie whispered something to her girlfriend then they smiled. Her girl laid me back and started sucking me while Tangie started riding my face.

It only took me about ten minutes of her gyrating on my face and she came everywhere. After that the both of them started licking her cum off my face.

They started kissing and I jumped in for a three way kiss session. That lasted a hot second then the other girl laid back and Tangie started eating her from the back.

As she ate her I slid behind her and started licking her pretty red fat ass five to ten minutes of that I was sliding rock hard dick deep down into her pussy.

The pussy was tighter that a safe and wetter than the ocean. Every time I thursted in and started to pull back she would grip my dick with her pussy muscles. After about twenty strokes I couldn't hold back anymore. I pulled out and shot my load all over her girlfriends face.

Tangie licked my nut off her face and once she was done her girl started shoving anal beads into Tangies ass. I pushed Tangies face down towards the dick and she knew just what I wanted.

As Tangie gave me massive head her girlfriend licked my ass. My eyes rolled to the back of my skull and my toes started curling.

I could feel my dick growing harder and harder in her mouth. The harder I became the deeper my dick was down her throat and the louder the slurping became.

I whispered between moans "that's it bitch suck this dick" I could feel her slob rolling down the shaft of my dick into the crack of my ass.

Soon as the slob reached my ass her girlfriend would quickly lick it up. I was so hard now I was ready to fuck again and motioned for her to straddle me.

She climbed on top of the pole and started twerking her tight little pussy to a slow rhythm.

Her girlfriend straddled my face and I instantly started sucking her sweet little pussy. Hearing the moaning from both of them at the same time instantly made me shoot my hot load fast.

Tangies girl started gyrating to the rhythm of my tongue and I knew that she was about to bust all over my face.

As she was releasing her nut all over my face she went into an uncontrollable shake. Soon as she finished her and Tangie started licking my face like two cats.

I had busted so many nuts that I couldn't think straight. All I could do was lay there and recuperate.

Twenty minutes later we were all in the shower washing each other up. I was getting turned on all over again so I quickly exited the shower as fast as I could.

I dried off and got dressed then headed to the door. As I was leaving I told them to hit me up and we would go for part 2.

Soon as I got into my car I rolled me a big blunt of purple and fired it up. I drove back to Nashville with a big smile on my face.

Soon as I past Bell road my cell phone started jumping for pills and coke so I headed straight to the Westside to collect my money.

Riding to that Jeezy it's the world cd had me super hype as I pulled up in the jungle. Since I was the only one with the work in the city it was only right to be listening to the song titled Escobar, because when I showed up on the scene it looked like I had hit a lick for about ten bricks.

I made a quick ten bands and kept it moving onto the north side to drop off some tabs and molly's than I headed to knock out wings on Jefferson Street. I ordered a twelve wing combo sweet tea and seasoned fries.

My order was ready within five minutes and I was out. I decided to go home and take a shower because I still had on my clothes from the day before.

As I came into the house I noticed my girl on the couch reading a book so I walked over to her and gave her a kiss on the forehead then asked her what she was reading.

She held the book up and said the Reaper Boys. I took a look at the cover and kept moving. I sat down and ate my food then headed straight to the shower.

I let the water run as I undressed, once the water was steaming hot I jumped in and handled my business.

As the water soaked my body I slide into deep thought about how was I going to get into the gated community out in Brentwood.

Soon as the idea hit me I exited the shower and quickly dried off. I ran to the computer and started looking at houses for sale in that neighborhood.

Soon as I found a few listings I went back downstairs and told my girl that I needed her to call a realtor and ask to view some houses.

She put her book down and started writing the info down on a piece of paper. I told her exactly what I needed her to do and she said ok. Soon as I finished giving her the details the phone started ringing.

I removed the phone from my pocket and answered it. To my surprise it was my big cousin Milan Mallory from the A.

I haven't heard from him in a while so I wonder what was the nature of the call so I got straight to the point.

"Yo Milan what's good cuz?"

"Trying to live but its hard now-a-days. Niggas hate to see you eating out here so before you know it they want to be you."

"Yea I smell ya, the heart can't stand what the eyes see."

"Exactly, Milian," said.

"How's Auntie doing?"

"Oh she's doing very well you should come up to see her, plus I need to run something by you that I think you would probably be interested to hear."

"Oh yeah then I'ma have to make my way over there. You know I never miss an opportunity to get paid or laid."

"Well there it is lil cuz, how soon can you come up?"

"Give me a week or so to tie some loose ends up down here and I'll be there."

"Ok see you then lil cuz, one."

"One."

Chapter 18

THE CAPTAIN HAD ASSIGNED me to the west sector of Nashville so I was happy. I was ready to clean up the streets and make a difference in the neighborhood. I knew my target area would be 40th Ave and the Jungle and my target people would be Brick Boy Mafia crew so I wasted no time making my presence known through all of west Nashville. I wasn't on the scene an hour into my shift when I spotted a guy named Catfish serving in the Jungle. After he served his customer, I watched him walk over to Obama's neighborhood market. I wasted no time pulling into the parking lot and jumped out of my car. I quickly ran into the store and slammed him down to the ground and started searching him.

Upon my search, I found a thousand of dollars and two pills and blunt of marijuana. The owner of the store was furious so I quickly got him to his feet and escorted him to the police car. Before the crowd began to get thick, I quickly confiscated the money, pills, and the blunt and let him go with a warning. I didn't want to waste my time with the paperwork, so I moved on the 28th and Swett's. Right way, I spotted a dice game over by the lil park, so I swooped in on them and caught them by surprise. A few ran, but I was able to catch a short black chubby male. Upon searching him, I confiscated a bag of Lortabs and a sack of crack. In the other pocket, there was a gun and three hundred dollars. I kick him in his ass a few times and then let him go with a warning. Just as I was walking back to my car, a Cadillac Escalade passed me with the music turned up loud, I quickly fell in behind it and pulled it over.

As soon as I walked up on the truck, I could smell the marijuana smoke. I drew my gun and told the driver to place both hands out of the window. I carefully watched the passenger as I handcuffed the driver and pulled him out of the truck. Once the driver was secured, I instructed the passenger to get out with his hands up. I quickly cuffed the passenger and went back to the driver. I asked him where the marijuana was and he replied, "It ain't no more, I smoked it!" I asked him if I could search the truck and he said, "No!"

As soon as I leaned over into the truck and started searching under the seat, I found a blunt of marijuana and a box of Swisher Sweet Cigars. I continued to search the vehicle for more contraband until I heard the driver yell, "Get the fuck out of my truck, pussy ass pig, there's nothing in there!" I moved on to the back seat area and made my move. I quickly stuffed the pistol and pills under the seat and called for back-up.

It only took five minutes or so for back-up to arrive, so I played it cool until the other units showed up. As soon as my back-up arrived, I quickly told them that I smelled marijuana and it's possible more is in the vehicle. The second officer joined in on the search and, "Bingo!" I heard him say, "Look what we have here."

He came out with the gun and the pills and the driver's eyes got bigger than golf balls. He instantly started yelling that it wasn't his. I quickly asked him, "Then whose is it?" My back-up looked at the other guy and said then it must belong to you. He quickly said, no no no, it's not mine. He said he didn't know what he was talking about. I started escorting them to the back of my police car and carefully put them in the back seat one at a time.

My back up called for a tow truck and I started filling out the report on the paperwork. Thirty minutes later, I was pulling into Davison County Criminal Justice Center. I quickly turned in my report and was on my way back to the dirty streets of North and West Nashville. While riding through the Northside, I decided to roll by 12th, 11th, 10th, Buchannon street, German town and Salem town. It didn't look like much was going on so I cruised over to the Bordeaux area. As soon as I arrived over by County Hospital area, I noticed a group of guys looking suspicious. I pulled over and started watching them. Ten minutes later a car pulled up and four of them took off running towards it. I watched them fight over who would make the sell. Before the first car pulled off, two more cars pulled up and they repeated the process.

I quickly rolled up on them and jumped out. AS I was exiting my car, they all took off running in different directions. I chased one of them through the neighborhood until he had nowhere else to go. I had him on the ground and I asked him why you ran. He said he ran because everyone else ran. I asked him where were the drugs and he replied I don't have any drugs. I removed some rubber gloves from my belt and put them on. "What are you going to do with those," he asked? I went straight in his ass crack and removed what I was looking for and he started screaming that I was violating his rights. I kicked him in his ass a few times and told him that he has the right to remain silent and the right to an attorney. Before I could finish reading him his Miranda Rights, he was begging not to go to jail. I stood him up on his feet and checked his pockets for other contraband and ID from his wallet. I removed all of his money and ID from his wallet. He continued to beg not to go to jail, so I asked him what he would do for me. I said ok tell me the names of the other three guys that ran. He gave me a bunch of nicknames so I told him that I want real names. He said he didn't know their real names. I told him that his ass depended on it and then started walking him to my police car. Upon arriving to the car, he gave in and gave me two names. I wrote them in my note pad and stuffed him on into the backseat. He pleaded over and over not to go to jail, but I took him anyway.

After taking him into the County, my shift was over, so I went home for some food and loving. Upon entering the house, I could smell the food cooking. I kissed Cookie and headed straight to the shower. The hot water poured over my sore and aching body and it felt good. I leaned over and let the hot water run down my back. Ten minutes later, Cookie was calling for me. I exited the shower, dried off, and got dressed. As soon as I made it to that table, I sat down to a wonderful Korean dish called Hangover Stew. I asked Cookie what was in it and she said beef broth, cabbage, bean sprouts, radishes, and congealed ox blood. I was little thrown off by the congealed ox blood, but I tasted it anyway and to my surprise, It was delicious. She explained to me that Hangover Stew was a dish that had been around since 1937 and I wasted no time digging into it. Once she knew I enjoyed the meal, she told me that she would make dish called kimchee. Without looking up, I said ok and continued eating until my bowl was completely empty.

After I finished eating, I decided to watch some TV so I started watching BET. Birdman and Lil' Weezy were sitting on the couch on 106 & Park. Baby was talking about his new vodka line called GTV and Lil Wayne discussed the details of his Trukfit clothing line. I thought to myself, "Damn them niggas have it all." I saluted to the TV and continued listening until my heavy eyes slowly fell shut.

The next morning started just the same as every day, except I wasn't running late today. I decide to run and check on the two names that I had written down on my notepad from the last night. One of the names on my list came back clean and the other one had a rap sheet, longer than Dickerson Road. I wrote down a possible address for the suspect and headed toward that location. When I arrived at the suspect's house, I parked and waited. An hour later, I decided to move on because I was bored and needed some real action. Just as I put my car in drive, I noticed a guy climbing out of bedroom window a few houses down. I put my car back in park and quickly jumped out. As I ran towards the guy, I drew my gun and ordered the guy to freeze. He took off running, so I chased him. The guy was Carl Lewis fast so I ordered him to stop and put his hands on his head. As I was running behind him, I stumbled on a tree root and my gun fired hitting him in his back. He fell to the ground, shaking and hollering. I called for back-up after I hand-cuffed him. When he was secured in the cuffs, I searched him for any weapons and contraband.

To may surprise, he only had a bag full of PlayStation 3 games. I cursed to myself and prayed like hell to come up with a good excuse of why I fired my gun. Before I could get my thoughts together, I noticed three other officers running toward me with their weapons drawn and I could hear the siren of the ambulance coming from a distance. A few moments later, the ambulance rolled up and two more police cars. My captain pulled up and asked me a few questions and then he handed me a cellphone. Before I could hang up with the Chief of Police, Channel 5 news crew ran past me with their cameras. I handed to phone back to my captain and he informed me to go straight in and file my report because Internal Affairs would need to see me.

I snapped out of my daze and I heard a woman screaming, no no no, why did he take my baby?!?! I watch as the paramedics pulled the sheet over his lifeless body and that's when I realized that shit had just gotten real. The news camera crew ran up to me, asking me ridiculous questions and before I realized it, I snapped. After I assaulted the Channel 5 news camera man, my Captain ordered me to get the hell away from the crime scene. I quickly walked pass all of the observers and shit talkers as I headed to my car. The mother of the child that I had just shot was now beating on my window screaming and crying.

A fellow policeman removed her from my path and I drove off. As I arrived back to the station, I was ordered to file my report and turn in my gun. The Chief wasted no time telling me that I had just shot and killed a sixteen year old boy. I dropped my head and shook my head. He told me that I.A would investigate the entire situation, but until then, I was to surrender my weapon and go straight on suspension with pay.

I was disgusted with myself. I called Cookie to tell her what happened. After calling to tell her and getting no answer, I decided to have me a few drinks to clear my head. I wanted to avoid everyone so I went to The Whisky Kitchen and got hammered. By the time the midday news came on, people started to ask me was I the cop from the news. I paid the bill and stumbled out to my car. I sat there another twenty minutes or so and then I pulled off.

Cookie started calling my cellular non-stop, back to back. I answered on the third attempt and she wasted no time with a lot of questions. I tried to explain, but she was so hysterical. As I was trying to calm her down, I ran straight through a traffic light and nearly hit an oncoming car. I told her that I would see her soon and I quickly swerved around a car that was in the turning lane and I went into an uncontrollable spin. I wrestled back and forth with the steering wheel until I finally gained control. I pulled into the Walgreen's parking lot to calm my nerves. As soon as I came to a complete stop, I leaned out of the door and threw up everywhere.

My phone started ringing and I reached between the seat to find it. I found it and looked at the screen and I answered it quickly. I heard my mom's voice and I broke down and started to cry like a baby. She tried her best to give me some words of encouragement, but it didn't help. All I thought about was the sixteen year old kid that I just shot and killed. I let my mom say what she had to say as I listened and cried in silence. I started to sober up a little and decided to drive on home and face my wife.

I entered the front door and Cookie was pacing around the living room. I took one look at her and I could tell that she had been crying. Before I could speak, I started explaining my side of the story. She cried even more and I reached out to her. I gave her a tight hug and a kiss on the forehead and then assured her that everything would be alright.

She started making a Korean meal, kimchee. I sat down in the recliner and waited on Channel 5 news to come on TV. Soon as the news came on, I was the top story. My stomach instantly balled up in a knot as I listened to the details. I became boiling hot because the news made me look like the worst cop in the entire city. My mind wandered off when the little boy's mother came on the screen. All I could think about was Internal Affairs and the lawsuit that she said she intended to file.

Before I realized it, I was sweating and my stomach was turning flips. I decided to take a cold shower to cool off. The shower turned out to be just what I needed. I dried off and headed towards the kitchen to see how much long it would be before my dinner would be ready. I sat at the table and talked to Cookie while she finished cooking the kimchee. As soon as she said that it was ready, I dug right into it before she could sit down and join me, I was done. She shook her head as I asked for another plate. She gladly prepared it and then sat down and ate with me.

We took our time talking and eating and then I helped her with dishes. After the dishes were washed and put away and we headed to the bedroom. I knew that she was worried for me so I assured her that everything would somehow blow over. As I reached for the night light, a sharp pain shot through my lower back so I let out a deep moan. She asked me what was wrong and I told her that my body was aching. She didn't waste any time telling me to roll over and lie on my stomach. She started rubbing my back down and it felt good. I buried my face into the pillow and closed my eyes. I mumbled a few words and before I realized it I was knocked out and into a deep sleep.

I was deep into a peaceful deep sleep when I heard the sound of my front door being kicked in. I jumped up from my sleep and quickly went for my Glock that was lying on the shelf in my closet. As I reached into the closet to grab my Glock, I heard the footsteps running down the hallway towards the bedroom. My wife screamed and I quickly spun around in her direction and that's when I heard the shots from go off. The bullet from the FNH 5.7 tore straight through my shoulder and it instantly spun me in a 360 degree circle. I dropped the Glock and fell over on to my side. A burning sensation rippled through my body and I nearly blacked out from the pain. As blood poured everywhere, I helplessly watched one guy smack my wife around like a ragdoll while another one tied her up to a chair. As I was going for my Glock, a third guy came through the door and shot me in the leg and I watched my leg get blown to the other side of the room. The third voice yelled out, for them to stop fucking around and help him with the big ass safe. The other two guys ran behind him and I attempted to crawl to my wife. By the time I made it halfway to my wife, I heard a crackling sound and the sound of something burning.

I realized that the entire apartment was burning. I fought harder to reach my beautiful wife. The smoke got darker and the flames got hotter and I became weaker and weaker with every breath. It felt like an eternity, but I finally reached my wife. Since my left shoulder was out of commission and my right leg had been blown off, I knew that I wouldn't be able to stand. I told my wife to rock her chair back and forth until she was able to tilt it over. After rocking several times, she fell over to the side and I used my good hand to free her. Once she was free, she said baby you have to make it because I'm pregnant with your child. My heart started beating faster because I desperately wanted to survive.

The faster that my heart pumped, the more the blood flowed from my wounds. I felt my body weakening, so I begged Cookie to please go. She cried and tried to drag me but my body was too heavy. I continued to beg her again and then I blacked out. Five minutes later, my body went into an uncontrollable shake and blood started pouring from my mouth and nose. Everything went black and my heart came to a complete stop.

Chapter 19

NIECY HAD DONE EXACTLY as I had instructed her to and we were about to close on the Brentwood house. I smiled to myself as I thought of the old saying, "If you can't beat 'em join them." I was anxious to complete the closing so I could take possession of the house so I could be in the same gated community as Eric. It wouldn't be long before his whole world would come crashing down.

Just as I was done with my packing, my cell started ringing. I looked at the screen and noticed that it was my momma calling. I thought, "What does this bitch want now?" I started not to answer the call but I decided to go ahead and answer. As soon as I answered, she wasted no time in telling me that Tre'Von was shot and burned up in a house fire. I almost dropped the phone when I heard the news. I instantly started to boil because I needed more details.

Shit sounded fishy to me so I quickly asked moms where was Cookie and she said Cookie was at her parent's house. Right away, I wanted to question her ass because that shit didn't sound right. I wanted to know why she didn't die and I was going to get the truth out of her if it killed me.

Three days later, I buried my brother and I was hungry for blood. As soon as the funeral was over, I approached Cookie and questioned her. She was happy to answer all questions that I had so that eased my mind a little after we started. I could tell that she was sincere and that she also loved him. As I stood to walk away, she called out to me so I stopped and looked over my shoulder. She told me that she was pregnant by Tre'Von and now he's gone and I don't know what I'm going to do. Not only did I lose him, I lost everything in the fire. I gave her a hug and I told her that

I would meet up with her before my trip to Atlanta. She shook her head okay and we parted ways.

I decided to give her the keys to the Brentwood house because I knew she needed somewhere to go. I stopped by the stash house and got one hundred grand and then started loading all of my bag into the trunk of the car. I called Milan and let him know that I was about to leave out and expect me to arrive in the A in less than three hours.

When I hung up with Milan and I got Cookie on the phone, we met up at Zaxby's on Bell Road. I bought me a chicken sandwich and some fries gave her the key to the Brentwood house and the one hundred thousand dollars and I headed down 1-24 East. I put my Webbie Salvage Life CD in and put the pedal to medal. About an hour out, I had to change CDs so I put that Yo Gotti in and continued jamming.

Once I arrived in Chattanooga, TN, I slowed down and took my time because I didn't want to be pulled over. I stopped and got a couple of Jumbo Buck scratch offs tickets and headed on my way. I decided to change CDs so I put in the Starlito & Don trip cd. As soon as the song Magic and Bird came on, I was in my grove. I cranked the music up a few more notches and headed on into Atlanta.

I quickly drove to Marietta Street and checked into the Omni Hotel at the CNN Center. I decided to pay for the park and pay package. The lady told me that it would be one hundred and eighty-four dollars per night and told her that I would be staying for three nights. I paid cash and headed up to my suite. I sat my bags down on the king-size bed and called Milan up. He answered on the fourth ring.

I wasted no time telling him which hotel I was staying in and he told me that I had made a good selection. He asked me would I be ready to meet in the morning and I told him yes. He told me that He would send a car over for me around noon and I said cool. We started talking about family and for a brief moment, I got quiet when he asked about Tre'Von.

I told him what happened and he gave his condolences. I thank him and then we hung up.

Since I was famished, I decided to get something to eat and see the city. I noticed Ruth's Chris was only a block away, so I decided to eat there. I ordered the biggest steak they had and a few sides and then sat back and waited. I got bored so I decided to bullshit around on Instagram for a minute or two. Before I knew it, my meal was coming out. I logged out of Instagram and dug right into my meal and when I finished, I ordered dessert, and then I left.

It was early and I decided to stop by Lenox Square and do a little mall shopping. My first stop was Macy's. I grabbed a few things for Niecy and then I headed to the Nike Store, Michael Kors, Louis Vuitton and the True Religion Store. After that, I was bored so I decided to chill in Peidmont Park. I got there and I sat down and rolled up a blunt of loud and relived my anxiety. After my blunt was finished, I stopped at the Underground to see what was happening. Niggas were everywhere and I felt right at home. I walked over to a store because I was curious to know what was going on with crowd of people. Once I got up on the crowd, I noticed a security officer arguing with a group of guys.

Without hesitation, the mall cop pulled out a Taser and shot one of the guys. Another one acted like he wanted to rush him, but he pulled out a Glock and told the nigga to get back. I thought, "Damn, that shit is crazy." The other two guys helped their partner up to his feet and the security officer continuing cursing and threatening them. I kept it moving because they were blowing my high. Since I was only a half block from my hotel, I decided to go back to my room and relax.

I arrived back into my room in less than ten minutes. I put my bags away and walked down to the spa area of the hotel Natural Body Spa. I paid one hundred dollars for a sixty minute massage. I laid back and let my body get some serious pampering. I nearly fell asleep on the massage table. Once my massage was over, I strolled back up to my room and laid back. Facebook was slow and boring so I logged into Instagram and played around for a minute. After an hour or so, my eyes became heavy and I blacked out.

The next morning I awakened to the sounds of the alarm of my iPhone 5. I quickly showered and I got dressed. I strolled down to the in-house restaurant called, Prime Meridian and ordered the buttermilk biscuit with gravy and the steak and eggs. I took my time and enjoyed the meal because it was delicious. Just when I realized that I didn't order a drink, my cell began to ring. I looked at the number and it was Milan. I quickly answered and instantly smiled from the news that I heard. I paid for my meal and headed out of the door as fast as I came.

When I stepped outside of the hotel, a Bentley Coupe was waiting on me. I couldn't; stop smiling the whole time as I walked toward the car. Once I got inside the car, the beautiful young lady introduced herself as Jamie. I instantly became rock hard. She must have noticed me re-positioning my crotch because she quickly said she was Milan's wife. I introduced myself as Je'Von, Milan's cousin and told her that I was pleased to meet her. Right away she explained that Milan sent her to pick you up. As we rode through Grove Park, heading to Bankhead, I stare out the window looking all of the nice houses. We drove in silence for a minute until she finally broke it by saying here we are. As we turned up in the long driveway of the house, I started thinking, "What the fuck is this nigga doing?"

As soon as the car stopped into the garage next to the drop head Rolls Royce. I said, "I know this nigga ain't living Fed like this." She showed the way to Milan and I was very impressed on how he was living. Once we reached the master wing of the house, I noticed a guy in a wheel chair. I thought this must be her brother. Maybe he's an ex-football player that was injured or something. When the fancy looking wheel chair swerved around, it was Milan. Without hesitation, I said, "Damn Milan, what's good cuz? What the hell happened to you?"

He thanked Jamie for bringing me and told her that she could excuse herself. I didn't want to seem like no groupie or nothing, but I excitedly asked Milan, "How in the fuck you living like this?" Milan smiled and said, "Yeah lil cuz, I see you like this shit. Man, this is just the tip of the iceberg. You haven't seen the whole iceberg yet." I said, "If this is just the tip, then I can't imagine what the whole iceberg is like."

Before, I could say another word, Milan yelled out, "Cold!"

I caught what he was saying and then burst out laughing. We started laughing. I could see that he still had his sense of humor, but I was still puzzled by the wheel chair. I looked around the room, smiled, and said, "Damn Georgia Boy, life must be good." He said, "Life is good, but all good thangs come with a price," he said. I said, "Yeah, I feel ya, but at this level of the game, it shouldn't be nothing but happiness."

"Je'Von," Milan began, "I'm glad you said that because happiness is part of the reason I called for you." I looked him in the face and I could tell that he was serious. I stopped smiling and asked, "What is it cuz, talk to me." Milan said, "I know you are wondering why I'm in this wheel chair." I shook my head yes and he proceeded to tell me how had become one of the biggest drug lords in Atlanta and his best friend Rico had got murdered. I listened as he told me about his plug and his beautiful soon-to-be-wife, Jaime. He talked non-stop for over an hour and then finally got to the part about his enemies, Danny Boy and Casper Jr. That lead to the wheel chair part of his life and right away I understood what was happening.

I asked him what he need from me because as far as could see, he had the whole world in his hands. As soon as I asked the question, Milan explained that he had a small problem named Jimmy Mason. He said Jimmy Mason was a FBI agent from Ohio that re-located to Atlanta to clean up the streets. He pulled a file on Jimmy Mason and handed it to me. I opened the file and started reading the newspaper clippings and the other documents on Mason. I read article after article on him and then I asked Milan what all of that had to do with me.

He said Mason was trying to build case on me, but one of his star witnesses committed suicide and Jimmy was trying to pin the homicide on me. I asked Milan what he needed me to do. Milan told me that he would make me a very wealthy man if I eliminated the problem. I thought about what he was saying and told Milan that I wasn't sure about it. I just wasn't sure about killing a federal agent. Milan promised that he'd make me a wealthy man. He looked me square in the eyes and said he would give me a half million dollars. I told him, I'm already worth that and I already had something lined up when I touched down back in Nashville. Milan then offered one million and a supply of one hundred bricks a month. I told him he was bluffing but he said it was real talk because he needed that nigga gone so he could get back to regular business of living and enjoying what he had.

The offer was looking real good. I knew with the Milan backing, I could compete with those Brick Boy Mafia niggas, so I told Milan I would do it but I needed to know what he was going to let me get the bricks for each month. He said twenty-six a piece and I told him he had a deal. Milan was glad that we could come to an agreement and he told me he had something for me.

He rolled away for a brief moment and then he returned with two cases, one was silver and one was black. I smiled cause I knew what was in the silver one but I wasn't sure of what was in the black one. He sat both down and told me they were both for me. I open the silver one and it was crisp stacks of one hundred bills. I opened the other case and it was a .308 sniper rifle. I told Milan that's what I was talking about.

He gave me a list of restaurants where Jimmy Mason and his wife were known to eat at and another list of information with his address, daughter's school, wife's work address, and maps of the city. He asked if there was anything else that I needed and I asked for full body armor and night vision goggles. He said he would get the items before the night was over. He threw me a burner phone and he said use this if you need to call me. I said cool and he called Jamie back into the room. He instructed her to give me a ride back to my hotel room. We left out the same way he came in and before I knew it, I was back in my hotel room a million dollars richer.

Chapter 20

I NEEDED A PLACE to stay because I didn't feel comfortable staying in a hotel with a million dollars in cash. With the help of Milan, I purchased a house out by the airport in the Camp Creek area. Every day I got up early and drove into the city to scope out my target and escape routes. I followed the same routine every day for a month straight until I was familiar with the entire city of Atlanta and Alpharetta, Georgia.

I followed Jimmy Mason and his wife to Bloomingdales in the north Point Mall. I watched them enter the store hand in hand like a couple deeply in love. I waited another five minutes or so after they entered and I leaped out of my car and made my move. I casually strolled through the parking lot like a tourist until I arrived at their car. I looked around to make sure no one was watching me and then I put a tracking device under their car and walked off. I got back in my car and activated the switch. Once I was satisfied that the device was working, I drove off and waited.

An hour later, they came out and got into their car. I popped in my Malaki, The Beast CD and took off behind them, staying five car lengths back. I followed them to the Alpharetta Athletic Club over on Dinsmore Road. They pulled in and started unloading their golf bags from the trunk of the car. I noticed two more vehicles pull up beside them. The occupants of both cars got out and they all started hugging and shaking hands. I figured they were probably federal agent's wives also, so I drove down to the east side of the parking lot and waited for the right time to make my move.

Three hours later, I got hungry so I went to get a bite to eat at Popeyes chicken. I ate my meal and then stopped and bought a hundred dollars' worth of scratch-off tickets. I sat in the car and watched a couple of thick bitches go in and out of Popeyes chicken until I noticed that my target was on the move again. I followed the signal on the device until I finally caught up with them. I was relieved that that the two other cars wasn't with them. I watched them pull up at Pappadeaux's Seafood Kitchen. I slumped down in my seat and waited. An hour later, they were walking out of the restaurant. It was turning dark so I became anxious and excited.

I followed them to the babysitter's house and watched them go in together. I knew it was only a matter of time before they headed home so I pulled off and headed toward their house. Twenty minutes later I noticed them coming on the tracking device. I pulled my Dodge Charger over to the right side of the road, but made sure my tail end blocked the driveway. I stuck the Glock 40 down in my waist and jumped out of the car. I lifted the hood on my car and waited. Five minutes later, Jimmy Mason and his wife pulled up. He rolled down the window and asked what seemed to be the problem. I told him that I wasn't sure, my car just stopped. Jimmy Mason put his car in the park position and got out to help. As he was walking up to me, I asked if would by any chance have a flashlight. He said he did and he turned to go back to his car. I pulled the Glock out and set off three rounds to the back of his head. As the sound of shots exploded, I watched his lifeless body fall to the ground. Before his wife could scream, I ran to her side of the car and released six through the passenger window. The glass exploded and she automatically slumped over in the passenger seat. I closed the hood of my car and gunned it down the block at full throttle.

Forty-five minutes later, I was back in the Camp Creek area of Atlanta. I pulled over and destroyed the tracking device and dumped the Glock. I pulled into my garage and broke down the 308 and neatly put it back into the case.

Five minutes later, I called Milan and told him to look at the news. I turned on the TV and the murder had made breaking news on every channel. I watched the news over and over on three different news stations. A spokesman for the FBI came out and spoke and then the Mayor. I sat back and laughed because it was funny to me. Soon as the news was done with that, they went straight into a story of the 30 Gang.

I laid low for a week and then I decided to head back to Nashville. Before I was set to leave, Milan called and said he wanted to see me. I waited for Jamie to show up and then I followed her back to Milan's house. When I arrived, he was in the back yard playing with a puppy. I said, "What's up Georgia Boy? What kind of dog is that?"

Milan responded, "This little fellow here is called a Japanese Akita. He's only four months old but you should see him when he reaches one or two years old. You know Jay, I love these dogs, and this is my second one. Before I got shot and before the home invasion ordeal, I had one of these same dogs. Boy I loved that dog. He was so smart and loyal to the point that he would take a bullet for me. But anyway lil cuz, I know you are wondering why I've called you here today."

I shook my head but before I could speak, he threw me the keys to a brand new Bentley Flying Spur and said, "I hope you enjoy this."

I told Milan, "Thanks cuz. This is a bad motherfucker. I can't wait to shit on them niggas in Nashville in this. They ain't gonna see this coming." We both started laughing and then I said, "Damn cuz, this here is love. I'ma show these bitch niggas how to get some real paper and I can't wait to burn the city up!"

"Oh yeah, speaking of burn the city up, give me the keys to the house in Camp Creek and I'ma take care of the Charger," Milan said.

"Yeah, I almost forgot about that. I tell you what cuz, I'ma drive the Bentley back to the 'Ville so can you just put this car in the garage when you remove the Charger?"

Milan responded, "Yeah cuz, I'll handle that and don't worry about nothing. I'll also have that first one hundred headed down to you in a few days so be ready for a snow storm."

"YEEEAAA, that's what I'm talking about, I'ma show these niggas who the real snowman is." I gave Milan a hug and told him thanks. I'll see you soon Milan replied, Jamie escorted me to the garage area pointed at the Bentley and said it's all yours. I put my million in cash into trunk of the car and rolled out. The whole ride home, I kept looking in the rearview mirror smiling because I couldn't believe I was about to be a made nigga. As soon as I crossed over the Tennessee/Georgia state line, I decided to get something to eat and fill up the gas tank. I bought some roasted chicken and two big potatoes then paid for my gas.

As I was about to start my car up, I noticed a red Ferrari pulled up. I turned the ignition on and started to approach the Ferrari. AS I approached it, it took off like a bat out of hell. A bright red light on the dashboard of my car came on and then a few seconds later a big explosion erupted and all I saw was a white light. The car explosion was so big it took out the Bentley and the entire Shell gas station.

A mile down the road, Jamie rolled down the window on the red Ferrari and tossed the detonation switch out of the window. She lit a cigarette and sped off back to the city limits of Atlanta, GA.

THE END